Heart
Shaped

Also by Siobhán Parkinson

Bruised

Shortlisted for the Children's Books
Ireland Book of the Year Award, 2012

Siobhán Parkinson

A division of Hachette Children's Books

First published in Great Britain in 2013
by Hodder Children's Books

1

A Catalogue record for this book is available from the British Library

ISBN 978 1 444 90360 7

Typeset in Bembo Book by Avon DataSet Ltd,
Bidford-on-Avon, Warwickshire

Printed and bound by
CPI Group (UK) Ltd, Croydon, CR0 4YY

Hodder Children's Books
a division of Hachette Children's Books
338 Euston Road, London NW1 3BH
An Hachette UK company
www.hachette.co.uk

To my fellow castaways, Elaina, Jane,
Rex and Valerie; Bill, Carrie, Ian,
Jean, Kevin, Paula, Roger and Tom

Beshrew me but I love her heartily;
For she is wise, if I can judge of her,
And fair she is, if that mine eyes be true.
And true she is, as she hath proved herself,
And therefore, like herself, wise, fair and true,
Shall she be placed in my constant soul.

The Merchant of Venice Act II, Scene VI

Nightmare

People are always saying things are a nightmare. The traffic is a nightmare. There are three people ahead of them in a queue, and it's a nightmare. The ATM only gives fifties, and it's a nightmare. They can't open their shoelace because it's knotted too tightly and they've cut their fingernails and that's a nightmare too. They don't really know much if that is their idea of a nightmare.

See, it is all green and wavy in my nightmare, like the fronds of some deep-sea ferns that are trying to entangle me. Even when I wake up, the nightmare still brushes at my ankles, because even though I know I'm not underwater now, there are worse things than ferns and weeds and drowning: there's being awake, there's having to get up and get dressed and go to school and deal with the Keith Butlers of this world, and the Toady Clarkes. And there are these black spaces in my head where I mustn't ever, ever,

ever go, because they are quicksand, and they will suck me down, and I will never be able to get free again, to live my life. I know that if I go there, I will spend the rest of eternity rolling in the blackness, hardly able to breathe.

But I want to breathe; I know I need to. So I sit on the side of the bed and I make myself draw long, slow breaths, expand my lungs, release the air, until the suffocating feeling goes away, until I can stand up and my legs don't tremble, and I can start putting on my dressing gown.

I couldn't tell Dr Thing about my nightmare. I couldn't describe it, because it's just a feeling. Nothing actually happens. I'd say head doctors love it if you can tell them about being chased by an axe-murderer in your dreams, or being on the bus and discovering you are naked or you open a window and somebody hands in a dead baby to you, wrapped in a sack. Having frondy feelings around your ankles and thinking you are a bit of an octopus is probably not very easy for them to work out what it means.

That is how it has been all my life. Or as long as I can remember, and I have got very good at it, at the long, slow breaths that draw me back from the nightmare, from the abyss, in the mornings.

But I should go back to the beginning. Or one of the beginnings, because where does anything start anyway? I suppose I mean, the point where everything started to go hell-shaped.

Chapter 2

Hell-shaped

Nobody answered when I rang the doorbell, and I didn't have a key. (No-key is my middle name.) There was a flyer for a takeaway pizza place jammed in the letterbox. It made the house seem deserted, as if nobody lived here, which was ridiculous.

I needed to go to the toilet. Now that I couldn't get in, this vague need had suddenly developed into a towering necessity. I looked around desperately at the neighbours' houses. Not a sinner. Not as much as a dog. Not a sound either. No garbled TV conversations from behind sealed windows, no children screeching, not a sign of a car or a bicycle on the road. I felt as if I was in an episode of *The Twilight Zone*, the last girl on a planet laid waste by some silent killer.

It was that dead time of afternoon. Maybe it's always like

this, I thought, when we're all at school. Maybe the whole estate goes into a kind of short-term hibernation, two hours of stupor, like in a Mediterranean country where they do that siesta thing.

Braiding my legs around each other – no mean feat when you are standing up – I banged on the knocker. Stupid. I'd heard the doorbell ding-donging. The house sounded hollow, as if . . . well, I said it already, as if nobody lived here. As if there wasn't even any furniture in it. That was ridiculous too.

Keeping my legs well knotted, I yanked the pizza flyer out of the sprung jaw of the letterbox and bent forward from the waist to squint through the slot. I don't know what I expected to see, because I knew there wouldn't be anything except the hall table and the stairs. Right enough, there wasn't anything to see apart from the familiar rickety table with the phone on it – one of those old-fashioned creamy-white ones with a receiver you could club a small child to death with – the hall was empty, dead, no sign of life. The faded picture of a duck-pond hanging above the phone table looked more faded than ever, the ducks gone all pondweed-green.

Now what was I going to do?

A bird twittered from a hedge and I jumped. At least it was

a sign of life. It turned a beady look on me and gave a little two-legged hop and disappeared into the undergrowth. I wished I could be a wee bird and pee in a hedgerow.

I stood back from the door and looked at the house as if I'd never seen it before, like someone casing the joint, looking for a weak point to exploit. I shifted my weight rhythmically from one foot to the other. The front-room curtains were closed, I noticed, which was odd at this time of day.

I went to the window, to see if I could find a crack to peer through, though I don't know why I thought that would be of any help. The curtains turned their sad beige lining to the front garden and there was a tear I'd never noticed before, a gob of lining hanging down, where a worn place had finally disintegrated. My heart gave a little lurch, my stomach clenched, and I leaked slightly into my pants. Oh, God. I leaned my forehead against the windowpane, to feel the calming cool of it. A bluebottle was trapped between the curtains and the windowpane. I couldn't hear the buzz through the glass, but I knew from its frantically pulsating wings that it was making a racket like a tiny helicopter.

I went around the back. Why hadn't I thought of that before? Force of habit, I suppose. The back door hasn't been used for years, not since that cupboard went in that was slightly too big and it blocked the way to the door, unless you are a stick insect. There was a doormat on the back step, all the same. One of those rubbery ones with gaps, and the gaps had all filled with dirt so that if you lifted the mat, there'd be a chequered pattern on the step.

But – hurray! – the bathroom window was open. It looked so inviting, I didn't think twice. There's a coal shed that is built right up against the house, a shed with a flat roof. I reckoned that if I could shin up onto the roof of the coal shed, maybe I could swing on to the bathroom windowsill and squeeze in that way. I have never fancied myself as Spiderwoman or She-Ra or any of those super-fit, super-agile, super-female super-heroes with super bladder control, but I managed it anyway. I grazed my shin and ruined the toes of my school shoes (pity, that!) on the climb up, but once I was on the roof of the shed, it was no bother to swing up and in the bathroom window. It shouldn't have been left open. *Anyone* could break in.

The bathroom was a mess, towels flung on the floor, over the side of the bath, loo paper unrolled in untidy streamers everywhere, as if there'd been a small storm in here, but to me it gave out blissful signals. I whipped my jeans down, jammed myself onto the loo and groaned with relief.

After I'd finished and washed my hands, I picked up the loo roll, rolled it back loosely on itself and fixed it into its holder. Then I folded the damp and knotted towels over the rail above the radiator and stepped out into the house. It was just as quiet inside as it had been outside. Silent as the grave. Even the air seemed to be holding its breath. And there was this weird sweetish smell, a bit like cider, which didn't make a whole lot of sense.

I thought of the bluebottle trapped behind the curtains downstairs. It would be daft to say my heart went out to it, but I did somehow feel I ought to open the curtains, open the window and let it out. *Ladybird, Ladybird, Fly away home*, though of course a bluebottle is much more repulsive than a ladybird, which isn't repulsive at all.

If the stairs hadn't been carpeted, my footsteps would have echoed all the way down to the hall, but they were, so they didn't. I was being melodramatic now, I knew.

Who the hell had left the bathroom in that state? I suddenly thought to ask myself.

The house was freezing. It's amazing how cold it can get indoors when it's February and grizzly outside. It felt as if the heating hadn't been on for weeks. I started towards the kitchen, to check on the boiler, but then I remembered I'd been on my way to the sitting room to release that stupid fly.

When I opened the door to the front room, a blast of

stinking heat hit me. The electric fire was blaring away, as if there was no tomorrow, and there was a hulking shape on the floor. I could just make it out in the grey light that filtered through the curtains and the red gleam of the electric element. *What the . . . ?*

I tiptoed closer. This could not possibly be happening. Not to me. Not *again.* Of all people, I could *not* be seeing what I was seeing. How could there possibly be a *person* passed out, or worse, on the living-room floor? In the middle of the afternoon. (As if the time of day could make a thing more or less likely. Not very logical thinking, I know.) Or maybe she was just asleep, on the floor, with a rug thrown over her, as if someone had found her there and thought she might get cold. Cold! The heat was like a thing you could touch.

My head started to swirl and the room started to shelve away from me, as if I were up too high, on the top of the Eiffel Tower or the Empire State Building. The bottom half of my body seemed to buckle back on itself, as if it was made of some malleable substance, like Fimo or Plasticine. I concentrated on not collapsing, but the effort made me feel sick. I put a hand out for support and leaned for a moment on the upright of the sofa. The velvet fabric of the upholstery felt slippery under my fingers, as if the very furniture was repulsing me. I could hear the muffled whirring of the bluebottle now, from behind the curtains, and my knees finally gave way under me and I folded to the floor.

I started to scream.

"Mammy!" I screamed. "Maaaaaaaaaaammy!"

I heard myself screaming, and I knew my mouth was open, but it didn't feel as if I was doing the screaming.

It was, though. I know because my throat was sore and raw the next day, as if an army of elves had spent all night working on it with sandpaper and Brillo pads.

I hear those screams in my dreams. I scream those screams in my nightmares – or try to, but as soon as I open my mouth, someone spreads a blanket over me and my airways fill with fabric. I'm breathing *stuff*, and my lungs turn to kapok.

So now you know.

Chapter 3

Holding Each Other Up

I didn't tell Dr Thing the *whole* story, of course. I definitely didn't say about leaking into my pants, for example. A girl has to have some dignity. But anyway, that's more or less what happened, as well as I can remember.

He coughed slightly, Dr Thing, as if to show he was still there. That made me realize I must have gone off into a reverie. (What a lovely word that is! *Reverie*. It makes me think of walking in a forest, with light coming filtering in through the leafage, making everything shimmery and shadowy at the same time, so you can't tell what's real and what's just an effect of scattered sunlight.)

I looked at him and wondered if I'd said something out

loud. I think I must have, because he was nodding, as if to say, *Yes, well, that figures.*

Good move, then, whatever I'd said.

"So do you want to tell me what happened next?" he asked.

Let me see. "The guards arrived."

"The police? Are you sure? How come?"

Why did he want to know that? I wondered vaguely. Probably trying to make sure I was thinking straight, I suppose.

But it was a good question. How come they *did* turn up? There I was, collapsed in a heap, beside . . . (oh, God) the *body* . . . and next thing I hear that scream that was different from my own scream, more like seagulls, and there's a blue light racing around the walls, racing and racing, around and around, and next thing I hear the doorbell being rung and rung and then the hammering of the doorknocker, *thud*, *thud*, and the snap of the letterbox. It was a weird sensation, like I had replayed a video clip of myself outside the door, only now I was on the other side of it, listening to the sounds from inside the house. Someone must need to use the loo very badly, I thought, and gave a hysterical little giggle. And then I think I passed out. It must have been the heat. Or the smell. Both, probably. And the shock, of course.

"How come?" he'd said.

Well, how would I know? I thought at first they'd come to investigate the . . . body. You know, like in a murder programme on the telly. In comes Lewis with his long face and that stupid look, and then there's fellows in white spacesuits everywhere. But it wasn't that, of course. I mean, nobody knew she was here, and dead, except me, and I'd only known for about fifteen seconds. In fact, I wasn't even sure, because no way was I actually going to *touch* her.

"Death follows me around," I said, not really to him. It was more a thought that just floated out of my mouth.

I closed my eyes.

Dr Thing said nothing. It was nice having my eyes closed and hearing him saying nothing. It was like a little patch of night-time, when you don't need to think or work. You can just be there.

After a while I opened my eyes.

Dr Thing nodded at me.

See, I was right, I told myself, about death stalking me. Even Dr Thing thought so.

I wiped my nose and looked out the window. The sky was grey and there were scraggy black birds gathered haphazardly on an overhead cable.

After a while Dr Thing said, "About the police, Annie? Did you want to tell me why they came?"

Did I want to? No, I didn't want to tell him anything. I didn't much want to be here. I didn't want to be talking to this Dr Thing at all.

I had nothing against him, don't get me wrong, nothing personal. But he seemed kind of irrelevant. I wanted to think about the idea of being stalked by death, and he wanted me to talk about this trivial matter of why the police had turned up.

I sighed and applied myself to his question. How come the guards had turned up, just at that moment?

"I think someone must have seen me 'breaking in'," I said after a moment, "and they must have reported it."

That made sense, now I came to think of it. Weird that things can make sense. It doesn't seem right. It should all be chaos, nothing should hang together, there should be no logic. Then really unlikely and awful stuff could happen and you mightn't notice how unlikely and awful things are. But unlikely and awful stuff in an otherwise ordered world – that's just wrong.

"Breaking in?" he said.

I laughed. Mirthlessly. It is not a nice word, that, is it? And it is not a nice feeling.

"Quick off the mark, weren't they?" I added. "Considering there wasn't a soul to be seen on the road."

He should have been the one to say that. That's how conversations go. But when you are talking to a head doctor, the rules of engagement are out the window. They don't say anything by way of conversation. They just ask the questions and write down your answers.

Mind you, this Dr Thing asked good questions – good for getting the facts straight in your head. The sequence of events, the causes and effects, the whys and the wherefores. Given that it's *not* a chaotic universe, that things do cohere at some level, then you need to make some kind of sense of it, don't you, if you want to keep yourself upright on the planet.

After that, my dad came. No, he didn't, that's stupid. After that, I must have been taken to the police station. I don't remember that part. I don't know why, either, unless they still thought I was a house-breaker.

I don't think I was unconscious or anything, I kind of half remember getting into the car, and someone had put a blanket around me, but not over my face, not so as I couldn't breathe, but I couldn't breathe anyway, and I realized after a while that I couldn't breathe because I was crying so much, the sobs and tears were fighting to get out of me, and there was no room left for the air to get into me. I thought I was going to suffocate. I wonder if you can die from crying? I never heard of it, but I can imagine that it could happen.

And then my dad came.

Oh, thank God, Dad came.

He came into this little room with no windows, where they had put me, with a policewoman to mind me. I couldn't tell you what she was like. I was hardly aware of her. It was as if everything was behind a kind of gauze curtain, the people all shapes, moving about in a grey haze, speaking to each other in some language I couldn't understand. I knew at some level that it was English, but I couldn't understand it.

I was shaking all over. I could see that my hands were trembling, and I could hear the chair I was sitting on shaking too, under me. Even my breath seemed to come in shaky little draughts and my teeth were chattering.

I couldn't remember how I'd got there. I couldn't remember anything except . . . *her* stretched out on the floor, and the smell and the heat. It was like a little piece of hell that I had just, sort of, wandered into.

It wasn't really *my* hell, I knew that. But hell is hell, no matter who it belongs to. The important thing to hang on to is that people can cope with hell. Everyone has a hell, but they are all walking around, taking the bus and reading the paper and digging their gardens and answering the phone and going to work and watching television and making fires and frying rashers and filling in passport applications and playing football, as if there wasn't any hell at all.

But you can't think like that at the time, when you just walk into hell and there it all is and you are fire-fighting. At that moment, you are just aware of the hell part. You've forgotten that you can cope.

My throat hurt. They'd given me tea, but it still hurt.

When my dad came into the room, where I was all hunched

on this wooden kitchen chair, I looked up to him. My shaking hand went to my throat, and I said, "Mammy!"

That was the first word I had spoken since I'd been found screaming by the police.

"It's your dad, Annie," said the policewoman who was minding me. I don't know how she knew my name. I didn't tell her. I don't know how they'd found my dad either. "Your *dad*."

I knew that.

But still the only word I could get out was "Mammy!"

Dad put out his two hands to me, and I caught them in my hands. He hauled me out of the chair and I fell against him and I wet all the front of his shirt with my tears and he was crying too, and we were holding each other up.

When we got home, Dad made me some more tea – I don't even like tea much, why do people always make you tea? – and French toast and he filled a hot-water bottle and went upstairs to put it in my bed, and then he came back downstairs and stood over me to make sure I ate a bit of the French toast, and then he sent me to bed. Poor Dad. There was no one to make tea for him and send him to bed. He just had to get on with it. If that's what being an adult is about, I think maybe I'd like to stay where I am after all, though being a teenager also sucks.

My dad is cool. I don't mean he's cool, as in cool dude. It's not that he wears the right brand of runners or anything like that. And I don't mean he's cool with stuff, like some parents let you do anything. But he's still a cool dad and I am so glad I have him. He doesn't do anything to be cool, he just is it, though there are some very theoretically uncool things about him.

He cycles everywhere, for example – he's very fit and wiry and he has one of those awful cycling hat thingies – and he plays chess. He taught himself, out of library books. Which is a bit sad, really, because you need two people for chess. He plays by email with some guy in Bratislava or Minsk or somewhere. I don't know if that makes it less nerdy or more nerdy. (I think I inherit my nerdiness from him. Which kind of makes it not so bad. It's not your fault if a thing is genetic, is it?)

A bargain is what Lulu Fortycoats used to call him.

She was an old lady who lived near us. Her nickname was Lulu Fortycoats because she used to dress funny, but she was dead sound. (Now she is just dead. See what I mean about death following me around?)

"Your mammy got a bargain there," Lulu Fortycoats used to say, about my dad, and Dad used to pretend to be embarrassed but you could see he was pleased, under it all.

He is a terrible cook, my dad. But he tries hard, and we have laughs, me and him and Jamie, about the awful messes he concocts. He cuts everything up so tiny when he is making pasta sauce, it's just this multicoloured *glumph*, like when a kid mixes up all the different colours of Play-Doh together and at first it's kind of stripy and cheerful but in the end it goes all brown and wormy-looking. That's what it's like when my dad cooks. Brown stuff that tastes like red stuff, i.e. tomatoes, because he always puts too much tomato concentrate in.

I was still in a daze. I just did what Dad said, got undressed and crawled into bed, and after a little while, he came and knocked on the door and said the doctor had come to see me. The doctor! Our doctor only makes house calls if you are dying.

But it wasn't our usual doctor, it was Dr Thing, the head doctor. That doesn't mean he is the boss doctor, it means he is a doctor for your head. I don't know how Dad got hold of him so fast. Anyway, he gave my dad some tablets and said I could have one if I couldn't sleep, and he would see me again in the morning.

Dad saw him out, and then he came and sat on a chair by my bed. I turned over and looked away from him. I couldn't talk.

Then I heard his voice. At first it was like the voices in the *Garda* station: I knew it was English but I couldn't make out the words, and then after a while I began to understand it. He said he was going to read to me.

I think it must have been that play we are doing at school, I can't remember what it is called, but it is by Shakespeare. He must have found my copy of it by my bed, where I'd been learning a bit from it before I went to sleep the previous night – which felt like about six months ago. Our English teacher is like that, makes us learn stuff off by heart, even if we don't know what the hell it is about. She says we will be glad when we are older. One of those things adults are fond of saying that don't make any sense. By the time we are older, we'll have forgotten that they said it, so we can't prove them wrong. Very annoying.

"In sooth I know not why I am so sad," Dad read, and his voice was like music. It didn't strike me at the time, but he could have been talking about himself. Only they were Shakespeare's words, of course, not his own, but they sounded very right coming from him. Poor man.

I remembered the name of the play then. *The Merchant of*

Venice. That was the bit I'd been learning. I'd wondered about 'In sooth', whether it has anything to do with soothing. I'd written this yellow sticky to myself to remind me to ask the teacher, and I'd stuck it onto the page. (OK, so I'm a nerd, I'm cool with that.)

"It wearies me," Dad went on. I felt myself drifting on his voice. ". . . you say it wearies you. But how I caught it, found it or came by it, What stuff 'tis made of, whereof it is born, I am to learn . . ."

I fell asleep.

I hadn't taken the tablet.

Remembering in Colour

I think maybe people are embarrassed if your mother dies on you. Well, tough. If you're the one it's happened to, embarrassment looks like a kind of luxury.

That is why I like Emma, who is my very best friend. She doesn't find anything embarrassing. She just takes everything as she finds it. That is so refreshing. Also, she is very generous with her hair straighteners. That probably sounds trivial, but the thing about generosity is, it shows a good nature. Mind you, she sometimes just skims across the surface of things. I mean, she doesn't always *get* it, about what's going on in my head. Though in a way, that's good. She can be a kind of normality check for me.

A lot of the girls in our class are all about being stars. They aren't actresses, they are never going to be in films, but they don't know that yet, and they are practising for when they are beauty queens or one of the participants on reality TV. You have to admire their optimism, Emma says, because she always sees the bright side of things and she has a kind nature, but I don't think they are being optimistic. I think they are deluded. And even if they did get to be celebrities, our classmates, I wouldn't think, *Well, there you go, I never thought they had it in them.* I would think, *If that is what it takes to be a celebrity, I think I will just stay in this here cave and never have to talk to anyone ever again.* Except Emma. And my dad. And maybe Dr Thing, who really is OK when you get used to him.

Dr Thing didn't come again after the first day. After that, I went to see him in his office. I sat there, my head feeling as if it was made of granite, looking at his beige carpet and beige furniture and beige table lamps. I thought of telling him his interior decorator needed a personality transplant, but then I thought maybe the neutral look had some psychological explanation, calming people down or something. Though I think there is a fairly clear line between calming and depressing.

He sat at his desk and I sat opposite him.

"Am I not supposed to lie down?" I asked him.

"You watch too much TV," he said, which I thought was a weird answer. I don't watch telly lying down.

Though I know he is not stupid. He's a doctor, after all. They have to go to university and everything. For years. And study skeletons and sinews and do biochemistry. All formulas, I'd say that is, and long words. It is funny how people think it is subjects like English where you get all the long words. They have obviously never looked in a chemistry book.

Subjects with really long/weird words

German (long)
Chemistry (mega-long, hard)
Geology (weird, with a lot of Zs)
History (not in general, but it so wins with antidisestablishmentarianism)
Geography (lots of unpronounceable foreign places)

Subjects with great short words

English (love, night, go, smile, you, heart, when, kiss, dead)

He kept wanting me to talk about my mother, Dr Thing. But I never talked about her. That was one way I coped with hell.

"I don't remember," I said. "My throat is dead sore."

But I do remember a bit. And sometimes I try to make memories for myself. Nice ones. Like, sometimes I try to imagine her like one of those women in the black-and-white movies my dad watches on Sundays in winter, with carved hair and a satin dress with a big orchid on it and a voice like a bell, wishing on a star. But it doesn't work, because she wasn't the glamorous type. The opposite, actually.

It's a funny thing about those black-and-white movies – they are in black and white, obviously, so you don't know what colour anything is, but when I think of one of those women with the voice like a bell in her satin dress, I know it's this kind of deep cherry red, and her lipstick matches it and her hair is kind of goldy, not blonde, not red, but yellowish, like gold. Someone told me once that we all dream in black and white. I don't really believe it, but maybe we do, and then when we *rememb*er the dream, we remember it in colour, like me remembering the old movies in colour, even though I know I only saw them in black and white. I bet there is some brain scientist somewhere who could explain that.

Dr Thing laughed when I said that. He actually laughed. I don't think he is supposed to do that, but he's human, not always the perfect professional. It was only when he laughed that I realized I'd said it out loud. I thought I'd only been thinking that part, doing the reverie thing again.

He looked at his notes, Dr Thing. I had this horrible feeling that he had a whole lot of information in there about me. Had he been *talking* to someone? About me. I didn't like that. It was probably only my dad, but I didn't like it. I don't like being talked about.

Once I heard my parents talking about me. They didn't know I was there. They were discussing something totally ordinary, like what time I had to be at school or whether I needed a new schoolbag or something, nothing personal or anything, but I went ape, overhearing them. It was the way they kept saying "she", as if I didn't have a name. As if I wasn't me. Just the sound of it, the shushing sound of "she" this and "she" that, like the wind in the trees, it gave me such a peculiar feeling of not existing. Which is weird, I know, because if I didn't exist, how could they be talking about me, but it was just the "she" thing, it made it not-me, somehow.

I mentioned something about being fourteen, and Dr Thing nodded, as if he knew already what age I was. Worst thing he could have done. More evidence that he'd been talking about me. *She's fourteen. Difficult age.* That stupid rubbish adults go on with. What is NOT a difficult age? Twenty-five? Forty-three? How old do you have to be for your father to stop thinking you are *difficult*?

He asked me lots more questions, but I stopped listening

after a while because I wasn't going to answer any more of them. I knew the answers to some of them, and I didn't know the answers to others and anyway I was tired. And I wasn't sure I trusted him yet, either. It was only the second time I'd met him.

He said I didn't have to go to school for a few days. He said I could have a sick note.

That was more like it, I thought.

"What'll I put?" he said. "What'll I say is wrong with you?"

I thought that was up to him. He is the doctor, after all. I shrugged.

"Lovesick," I suggested, for a joke.

Not very funny, I know. There's a kind of joke you make when there is something you can't bring yourself to talk about, but you'd like to talk about it all the same. Dr Thing must have thought it was a real joke, because he laughed again.

"I'll put sore throat," he said. "If you'd prefer."

I suppose he meant if I'd prefer that to head case. Though possibly he meant to lovesick.

I *was* lovesick, though. Heartsick.

And Jonathan Kinahan was the cause of my grief. In more ways than one.

Chapter 5

Disappeared

OK, I realize I need to backpedal a bit, because I haven't mentioned Jono before, have I? Dr Thing was right. It is important to get the sequence of events sorted out, because otherwise nothing makes sense, or it makes the wrong sense. I mean, you can easily jump to the wrong conclusion.

Jonathan (also known as Jono, in fact, mostly known as Jono) was supposed to be my boyfriend. At least, Emma supposed it. (She's very optimistic, Emma.) I didn't suppose it, but I did wish it. (Oh, how I wished it!)

Back in the good old days, before I'd even heard of Dr Thing, I actually used not to think death followed me around. I was still living a fairly normal sort of life. Only Jono and I were going nowhere. Fast. Which was definitely not good, so it wasn't really the good old days after all. The good old days are a myth, if you ask me.

Right, well, I'll describe Jono, then. Because I like describing him. And because he's gorgeous.

He's tall (not just taller than me, actually quite tall, even for a boy) and he seems to have more elbows than most people. And there's a bit of his hair (which is just ordinary brown) that won't lie down – it's like this feather he's stuck into his scalp, at the crown of his head. His face is quite long, and when he smiles, he gets these two parallel creases down the sides of where his cheeks would be if he had cheeks. If his face was rounder, they would probably be dimples, but there isn't room for dimples on his face, just the creases. His eyes are navy blue, like a baby's, but he is not a babyface. His shoulders are narrower than they should be, but not, like, sloping or anything. There's room to put your hand on one of them, if you were at the putting-a-hand-on-the-shoulder kind of stage in your relationship with him.

Which I was not. Sadly. I was only at the 'Hey, Jono, how's tricks?" kind of stage. We had laughs together. We sent each other cute little texts. But we were still a bit shy when we actually met. We'd never kissed or anything. God, no. We were mates, me and Jono. Friends.

Anyway, back then, Emma used to try and bolster my confidence and tell me that "any day now", Jono and I would "get our act together" and there'd be kissing and swooning and sunsets and bluebirds twittering pretty little love-songs and everything would be rosy in the garden. That didn't happen, but it was OK, because there was always the prospect that it was going to happen soon.

Only then I began to notice that Jono wasn't around. He's in the same year as me, but we're not in the same class group, so I don't always see him at school every day. And he'd sent a text to say he'd be out of school for a while, so I thought nothing of it at first.

The cheery little texts kept coming, over the next while, but there was no sign of Jono himself coming back to school. I kind of wondered a bit, but it was none of my business. I once heard a teacher describing him as 'troubled', which is grown-up-speak for someone who skives off school. It doesn't bother me, though, that sort of thing. I mean, I'm not an adult, am I? They get so worked up about stuff that is really just nothing.

"Of course it's your business," Emma said. "You're practically an item, you two. Why don't you ask him where the hell he is?"

But I didn't. We weren't an item. Not even "practically" one, whatever that means.

The next thing I noticed, though, was that Jono's little sister

Julie was missing too. She goes to the kiddies' school, she's only young, but I often see her coming out of school when I'm on my way to band practice. That's in the community centre at the opposite end of town from our school.

We'd been having a lot of extra practices, because we were giving a concert in an old folks' home (the bandmaster says, ho, ho, ho, that it is a form of elder abuse). So there we were the other day (this is before, you have to remember, *before* Dr Thing and everything), me and Emma and a gaggle of us all clattering along the road with our instruments (I play the clarinet and so does Emma), and we passed Julie's school as the kids were coming out, and there was no sign of her.

"That's the third time we haven't seen her," I said. "Do you think something is wrong, Emma?"

Something was *bloody* wrong, but I didn't know that at the time.

"Yes, well, I suppose, Julie is hardly mitching," Emma said. "At her age."

"Exactly."

I like Julie. She reminds me of myself. So you can see why I couldn't just shrug it off that she'd disappeared. Or gone to ground.

"You could be right," Emma said. "Maybe something really is wrong. I think you should ring Jono, Annie. That'd be my advice."

She likes giving advice, Emma. I love her to bits, don't get me wrong, but I have to admit that there are times when I could cheerfully strangle her.

"We don't ring each other," I said. "We text."

Though that is not entirely true. Sometimes he phones me in the evenings. Used to phone me, I mean.

Emma rolled her eyes. She looked as if *she* wanted to strangle *me*. I don't know why.

"Well, *text* him, then," she said.

"I have done. I do."

"And has he texted back?"

"Yes."

"So he's not really all that missing, then, is he?" she said, all sweet reason.

"Except in the sense that he actually *is* missing," I said. "As in, nobody knows where he is. Nobody has seen him for ages. But I know he's not dead, I suppose. I give you that much."

"Oooh-oooh, moody!" she said. "So what has he got to say for himself?"

"That's the thing. He never mentions being out of school. He just sends these cheerful little texts. Football. Jokes."

"That's weird," said Emma.

"Exactly," I said again. "Considering I hate football."

It isn't even really that I hate it. It's just that I am totally indifferent to it, immune to it, you might say. I haven't a clue about it. They are always going on about the cup. As far as I am concerned, it might as well be the saucer. I don't know why it has to be about crockery. The cupwinners' saucer, that would be kind of cute. The fact is, I'd rather *knit* than watch football. And I don't even know how to knit. (I wish I could, actually, because I would love a polka-dot cardigan, and you just don't see them, do you?)

But anyway, that's not the point.

"No, you dolt," said Emma, "*considering* he and Julie have both been out of school a good three days by now, and not a squeak of an explanation."

"Yeah," I said, uncertainly. "Though he did say *something* a while back . . ."

"What sort of something?"

"He said he wouldn't be around for a while."

"Why? Did he say why?"

"God, Emma," I said, "I don't keep tabs on him. I'm not his minder."

"No, but, you'd think . . ."

"He *said* . . ." I said, but I couldn't actually remember what he'd said.

"Check your phone," Emma commanded, all detectivey, leaning over my shoulder.

I thumbed listlessly through my text messages. (Liverpool's chances in the cup. *Liverpool?* What makes him think I have the remotest interest in some city in England?) Some joke about a man who goes into a pub with a frog on his forehead. Some joke about a frog who goes into a pub. More about Liver-blinkin-pool.

"There!" Emma jabbed at the screen. "That's the one."

> Dear Annie, I won't be around for a few days. My ma has that vomiting thing. She's puking her guts up. I'm afraid she might faint or something, fall down the stairs or whatever, so I think I'll stay home for a while and keep an eye on her. I'll phone you tonight after the match. J

Dear Annie. He is such a goof-head, Jono. There can't be another person on the planet who puts *apostrophes* in text messages and starts with "Dear so and so". It's a wonder he didn't end it with "Yours sincerely".

"Hmm," said Emma. "So *did* he phone you after the match?"

"No," I said glumly.

"And you're worried, aren't you?"

"Ye-ah," I said.

"So *phone* him," she said. "I mean, you deserve an explanation."

"Do I?" I said. "I'm not his year head or anything."

"Oh, don't be stupid, Annie, you're his *girlfriend.*"

"I'm not. Not really."

"Well, you will be. You're in the early stages, that's all."

Which is exactly why I didn't feel he owed me an explanation. I'm just his text-friend. (He doesn't do Facebook. Boys aren't as keen on that as girls, I've noticed. And he definitely doesn't Tweet.)

But really I did kind of want to know what was going on, especially with Julie being out as well, and Emma kept banging on about how I should ring him.

"Look, Annie, this whole thing is really eating you up, and there is no point in being eaten up, you have to find out where you stand, what the story is." She likes these efficient little phrases, "where you stand", "what the story is"; she likes everything sliced and diced. "So my advice is you ring him and put yourself out of your misery."

My misery.

It seemed like really sound advice, like you get from those sensible people in magazines, agony aunts. But maybe I *liked* my misery. My nice, safe, why-doesn't-he-ring misery. Maybe I liked that misery better than I would like the kind of misery it would be if I rang him and it turned out he didn't give a damn about me and told me so. That really would be misery, I thought. And I didn't want to give him the ghost of an opportunity to say that.

I didn't know what misery *was* then. Because this was all way back. A good, oh, twenty-four hours, anyway, before my world went into free-fall and I started spinning and whirling and feeling as if my lungs were made of something you stuff cushions with.

"You're going to have to ring him," Emma was saying. Again. "Ask him what's going on. Maybe there's some sort of *crisis*. He said his mother was sick, didn't he? Maybe it's, like, *serious* . . ."

She made it sound like the Famine or the Plague or something. She can be a bit dramatic, Emma. (Though even Emma couldn't have predicted what actually *was* going on, not in her wildest dreams, because of course this was all *before* that day I *found her*.)

"I can't," I said. "I never have. The girl can't be the first one to ring."

Emma laughed. She said I was out of the Middle Ages.

I couldn't phone him, though, I really couldn't.

And then everything went hell-shaped, and after that it felt like it was too late.

"So what are we going to do about Jonathan *now*?" Emma asked then. I mean, after all hell had broken loose, and it didn't really seem to matter any more about phone etiquette.

I didn't know what to say. I didn't know what to do.

Chapter 6

Harassment

I think it would be nice to be in the Middle Ages, actually. There is this great statue kind of thing, a gravestone or something, in St Patrick's Cathedral (we went there on this school tour when we were in primary school) and it is to Lord Somebody and his family, and it has all these girls on it, his daughters, they all look like Holy Marys, but they have this great hair, down to their knees, nearly, and it is all wavy, as if they plaited it at night. It is the Middle Ages, I think. You could wear your hair all wavy in those days – you didn't have to have straight hair, the fashions were different then, and you would have knights singing love-songs to you and fighting jousts like in Robin Hood, and people like Keith Butler would be put in the stocks on the village green and we could throw rotten tomatoes at them. I like the sound of that. They probably didn't have tomatoes in the Middle Ages, but it could be oranges or Brussels sprouts.

I forgot to say about Keith Butler. He is this creep that was always stalking me at school. Fancied himself something rotten, and thought I should too. Emma said I should report him for harassment.

The thing about the Middle Ages, the rules would all be clearer, and there would be no mobile phones. You wouldn't have to be wondering if it is OK to phone someone who is not phoning you. And harassment hadn't even been invented.

I decided to tell Dr Thing about Keith Butler. Not because I needed to 'get it off my chest' or whatever the psycho-people call it, but because it was easier to talk about than all the mother stuff he kept wanting me to do.

I did *not* want to talk about *her*. It was all too complicated, and anyway, I hadn't worked out what I thought. She wasn't a bad person or anything, I wouldn't like anyone to think that, but she had her issues, you know?

That's what people say when they don't like to say that someone is a head case or an addict or a criminal – they say they "have issues". You hear the psycho-experts on the radio – the old people's station, with all the talk on it – banging on about people's *issues*. Not that my mother was an addict or a criminal or whatever, that's not what I mean. Oh, God, I keep saying the wrong thing.

Or thinking the wrong thing.

Sometimes I think it was all my fault, and sometimes I think she just wanted me to think it was all my fault, and then other times I think, that is a terrible thing to think about your mother, but maybe it's right, and just because it is a terrible thing doesn't make it not true.

But I'm not going to think about that. It makes me have those nightmares with the undersea fronds and not being able to breathe, and I do not LIKE that.

"There's this boy at school," I said, to Dr Thing. "I won't tell you his name."

He stopped twirling his pencil. He always has this pencil on his desk, and he twirls it while you are talking, and if you say something interesting, he stops twirling it.

"Like him, do you?" he asked.

"God, no. The opposite."

He frowned. I knew he was thinking that I meant I really did fancy him. That I was doing an Elizabeth Bennet hating Mr Darcy on it. How wrong could a man be? Head doctors don't always get it as right as they think they do.

"No, really," I said. "It's not that. It's not that *I* fancy *him*. I think it's more that he sort of . . . I mean, in this twisted sort of way . . . It's . . . it's like he's *stalking* me."

He started twirling the pencil again. I didn't know what that meant.

"Emma says it's harassment. You know . . . eh, *sexual* harassment."

I felt awkward saying the S word.

The pencil stopped again. I think he must have picked up that I was a bit embarrassed, because he said, "Are you sure you want to tell me about this, Annie? Would you prefer to talk to a lady?"

A *lady*! I burst out laughing. It was such an old-fashioned word, made me think of a woman in crinoline with a Marie Antoinette bird's nest hairstyle. Or maybe just with those old-fashioned 'nylons' with the seams up the back and extremely red lipstick. Like, *extremely*.

"No," I said, and suddenly I meant it. I didn't mind telling him after all. "You'll do."

So I told him the Keith story.

It began the day Jono sent me that text message, actually, the one about his mother being sick. I was standing in the classroom doorway before class began. My head was bent over my phone. I was really glad to hear from him, because I'd been wondering if everything was OK. And it seemed it was. He was just out of school, he said, because his mother was sick.

Anyway, Keith Butler came shouldering past me into the classroom. It's not a narrow doorway or anything, there was plenty of room, but he sort of stumbled up to me and leaned against me as he passed, as if we were trying to squeeze into a lift or onto a train or something. Weird behaviour, he practically mashed me against the door jamb. He mumbled something in my ear, really close and breathy. It might have been *Sorry* or it might have been *Get the hell out of my way* but I have to tell the truth and say I think it sounded like *Got the hots for you.* It's hard to tell with him. His tongue seems to be stuck to the roof of his mouth. I suppose that could really be true, it might be a *condition*, but, hey, I was not about to try to find out. Oh, yuck and double yuck. Keith Butler with the hots for me – it made me blush, and not in a nice way.

"Maybe you're right," I said to Dr Thing, blushing some more. "Maybe I shouldn't be telling you this."

"You're doing fine," he said. "You can tell me anything you like. That's why I'm here."

He must have got interested. Five minutes ago he'd wanted to fob me off on some theoretical *lady* head-doctor person. Oh well, I'd started now, I might as well keep going.

He used to be in our band, Keith. He once suggested to the band master (that word always makes me grin, I keep imagining a person with gold braid and epaulettes and brass buttons, like in the Salvation Army) . . . So where was I? Oh, yes, Keith suggested to the bandmaster that we call ourselves The Full Monty, which makes about as much sense as The Turnips or The Traffic Cones or The Cutlery Drawer or Brief Encounter (that is a movie, one my dad likes, an old one, but I can't tell you if it is in black and white or not because of this problem I have with remembering everything in colour).

This was all because I'd said I didn't think Convent Road Band was a very good name. I mean, Convent Road is bad enough as a street name, but as the name of a band, it really sucks. I thought of The Rubber Band, only a real group stole that name, or sort of did, so then I thought of The Hair Band, but the boys wouldn't go for that, I'd say. You always have to think about the boys, they have all these sensitivities, especially ones that do girly things like play in a band that is not a rock band. You have to make sure you don't seem to think they are girls' blouses. Though I don't see what is wrong with girls' blouses, but it is supposed to be a terrible insult.

Anyway, the head honcho, by which I mean the bandmaster, got very exercised about it, which was of course exactly why stupid Keith made the suggestion in the first place, just to rile him, and to embarrass the girls – embarrassing girls is his hobby, I think, but he doesn't have to do anything. His just *being* there is enough to make *anyone* embarrassed.

We never did find a new name. It's still called Convent Road Band. How sad is that? But at least it hasn't got the word 'youth' in it, which is good because that always sounds like a put-down. I don't mind 'young'. Like, Young Scientists is all right. But Youth Orchestra and Youth Parliament, oh, puke.

And then, Keith did the shouldering past thing again the next morning, only worse. I was standing in the doorway as usual, watching to see if there was any sign of . . . well, anyway. And he comes plunging out of nowhere and practically smashes my head off the door, and this time it's more than husky words in my ear, this time it's hands all over me, right there in the classroom doorway. I feel like I'm being frisked or something, hands everywhere and just as I open my mouth to protest, there's a big cold damp meaty hand over my mouth and the other one down the back of my neck and my head is slammed against the open door, and then he takes away the hand from my mouth and – well, I don't really want to describe the next bit, but, listen, it was wet, and I didn't like it. He gives me the creeps, and he smells sweaty.

The first time I ever kissed a boy I was twelve, maybe nearly thirteen. (I didn't tell Dr Thing this part, because it's private.) He was about sixteen, the boy, or maybe fifteen, but he seemed very grown-up to me. And I didn't like it all that much, but at least it was kind of exciting at the same time as being a bit disgusting, because he was, well, clean, for a start, and he had nice eyes and he smiled at me, but this was just disgusting. I wouldn't call it kissing, though, because kissing is nice, like you kiss your mam and dad, or your doll when you are small, or you kiss someone you fancy. This wasn't like that, it was more like drowning or choking or something.

"If Jono was here, I'd get him to fight Keith," I said.

"Who's Jono?" asked Dr Thing.

Oh. My. God. I shouldn't have mentioned his name. I never meant to.

If he could have stopped twirling the pencil, he'd have

stopped. I know, because he gave it a puzzled look. But he'd already stopped, so he couldn't.

"A boy in my year at school," I muttered.

"Another one?"

"Well, there's more than one, obviously." I sounded snappish, I know. Bad move.

The pencil started up again. "Go on."

So I told him how Mr O'Connell, who teaches English, saved my life. Or at least my virtue, or whatever you called it in the Middle Ages. He was passing, on his way to his classroom, and he saw Butler practically *raping* me in public, and he hauled him off me and started shouting at him in a very un-Mr-O'Connell-like way, because he is usually very softly spoken and you have to bend your head if you are on the tall side, like I am, or his words just float past you at about chest height and disappear into your jumper, and you haven't a clue what he has said. And it's sometimes important, so that is not good.

Anyway, he stood there holding Keith's jumper by the scruff and he's shouting about *school policy* and *inappropriate* (teachers love that word) *behaviour* and *sanctions* (that's another favourite, and it sounded very good to me too). So the upshot was that Keith was sent marching off to the principal's office for a talking-to and whatever else. Mr O'Connell said it was sexual harassment, which was what Emma had been saying all along, so I suppose he is right, but I would just say it is Keith being Keith. Though the thing is that being Keith is all about being a bully and a harasser and a stalker and all those things.

I was glad to be rescued. But at the same time, I wish it hadn't been Mr O who turned up just at that moment. If one of the lads had pulled Keith off me, it would have been better – imagine if it had been Jono! Only of course there was no sign of Jono – because now Keith was in trouble, and Keith doesn't like that. When Keith is in trouble, somebody has to pay.

"I see," said Dr Thing.

"For 'somebody' read 'Annie Walsh'," I said.

"Dear me," said Dr Thing.

I never heard anyone saying that since Lulu Fortycoats died.

Thinking of Lulu F made me remember Jonathan again – not that I needed to be reminded, I never did stop thinking about him – because of course she was his grandmother, and I keep remembering her when I hear old-person talk. It makes me smile when I remember her but it makes me go a bit teary too, she's not long dead.

"And?" said Dr T.

And.

"And now I had Come to the Attention of the Authorities," I said in a hollow voice.

"Not good?" he said sympathetically.

"Not good."

Chapter 7

Toad of Toad Hall

The Keith Butler story got more complicated after that, but I didn't tell Dr Thing this part, because it's only what goes on at school, it's not very psychological.

Mr O'Connell took me aside after class that day, back then when it happened. I say "back then", though we're only talking last week, really. But so much has been going on, it feels like ancient history by now. It's nearly like looking back on my childhood, innocent days.

Mr O'Connell said the principal wanted to see me. I thought maybe the school was afraid I was going to take them to court or something, because of Keith. Of course I hadn't a notion of doing any such thing. There really wasn't any space in my life for getting involved in a feud with the Butlers – which is definitely what would happen if I squealed on him to The Toad, so I'd decided to take the line that Keith had just got a bit overexcited and lost the run of himself. I didn't like it, but, you know, *Worse things happen at sea*, as Lulu Fortycoats used to say. I don't really know what the sea has to do with it, but I got her drift. She also used to say, *It could happen to a bishop.* That means it's not your fault, roughly. Which definitely doesn't apply to Keith, in this case. And not really to me either, because I can't imagine that happening to a bishop, can you?

So anyway, Mr O'Connell was just about to come in with me to see the principal, only then someone rang him on his mobile and he gave me this little wave, to say, *Go ahead, you'll be grand.*

So there I was arranging this smile on my face, all set to say, *Look, I appreciate your concern, but I'll get over it, don't be worrying*, when I suddenly realized that that was not what The Toad had in mind at all. He'd got the whole thing arseways. I bet he never listened properly when Mr O'Connell told him the story. He thought it was all *my* fault. I was just sitting there and he was going on with all this talk, I couldn't follow the half of it.

I couldn't get a word in edgeways to tell him it had nothing to do with me. I was only *there.* I did nothing (I was the bishop), but listening to him, you'd swear it was all my fault, that at the very least I'd led Keith on. He kept going on with all this stuff about how school policy prohibits, I dunno, prohibits something or other, something to do with sexual something, and how I had been in breach of something, rules I suppose or *protocol*, I think he said protocol, I thought that was for embassies.

I was flabbergasted. There I was all set to say it didn't matter, I wasn't going to make a fuss, and now it was suddenly all about *me*.

"I didn't . . ." I started to say.

But he didn't want to know.

"Were you or were you not kissing a boy in the classroom doorway this morning, Miss Walsh? Mr O'Connell informs me that you were."

Miss Walsh! I had never been called that before.

"No," I said. "*He* was kissing *me*."

The Toad stood up like a shot and leaned across his desk, so that his tie was hanging down and draping onto a pile of books, and he spat something at me about splitting hairs. Hairs! I wasn't splitting any hairs; I was only trying to explain.

I wished Mr O'Connell had come in with me.

"Young What's-his-name, Butler, yes, Butler, he has a different story," said the principal. "I spoke to him earlier, and I must say he gave a very convincing account of himself."

Was this the same Keith Butler I knew? The one whose tongue is stuck to the roof of his mouth?

My own mouth was hanging open.

"I am determined," Toady Clarke was raging on, "to nip this kind of thing in the what-you-call-it, the bud. In the BUD! Do you understand? Young Who's-it . . ."

"Butler," I muttered. "Keith."

"Yes, thank you. He tells me you brushed up against him in the doorway. Says you have been stalking him for weeks, constantly trying to get his attention. Give him no peace."

Stalking Keith Butler! Me? I nearly choked.

"What have you got to say for yourself now, Miss Walsh? Were you or were you not locked in an embrace with this – eh – Keith Butler?"

"Locked," I said. "That's what it felt like, yes. Locked. I felt as if—"

"We are not interested in how it *felt*, Miss Walsh." Whoever "we" was supposed to be. "You will keep your *feelings* to yourself. This is a disciplinary matter, not a psycho-what's-it. Do you understand?"

I am beginning to see the psycho-what's-it stuff in a different light. Dr Thing would have been proud of me. Except I wasn't seeing Dr Thing then, because that was before – you know it – all hell broke loose.

"No," I muttered, but he took no notice.

And then he was going on about how this kind of thing is contrary, "*expressly* contrary" to something. You'd think he had been practising these words all his life and had finally found an opportunity to use them.

"Expressly contrary to school regulations. It undermines the reputation of this school, a reputation we hold dear. Very dear. This school's fine reputation. Do you understand?"

He was dead keen that I should understand stuff. I know what I understood. The school is more important than its pupils.

I had all these words in my head, about how I hadn't intended to make a fuss about Keith but now I thought I might reconsider, but of course, I couldn't get them out of my mouth. I just slumped in my chair and muttered. I was your classic teenager in trouble at school. Only I wasn't in trouble. Not really, I couldn't possibly be. I had done nothing, absolutely nothing, and nobody could prove that I had. Could they?

"Good," he said. "That will be all. I will draw a veil on this occasion, overlook, you know, but don't let me . . . I don't want to hear . . . Just watch your step, young lady. And are those regulation earrings?"

I fingered my earrings. They are tiny silver hearts. Nobody could possibly . . . well, actually, anything is possible in this madhouse.

"Yes," I said, "they are regulation earrings. Regulation metal, regulation size, regulation type. But they are heart-shaped. I hope that is not against the regulations?"

"Heart-shaped," he repeated, as if he really was considering whether heart-shaped earrings might be some sort of breach of discipline. "Hmmm."

"They are purely decorative," I said. "The hearts, I mean. They are not meant to be some kind of a romantic signal or anything. You don't think they could possibly . . . oh, dear, Mr Clarke, it couldn't be that you think wearing hearts in my earlobes is a kind of come-on, do you? Because if that is the case, you should definitely consider banning heart-shaped things, if they drive the boys wild, I mean, they might be dangerous."

I was pushing it, and I knew it, but he's such a nincompoop, I figured I could get away with it. And he deserved it.

"What?" the principal bellowed. "What did you say?"

"Nothing," I muttered.

"Go back to your class, Miss, eh . . ." said Mr Clarke, otherwise known as Toad of Toad Hall. (His real first name is Thady. Well, I mean . . . come on, irresistible.)

I looked at my watch. "It's half past four," I said.

"Well, go home, then, you know what I mean."

I met Mr O'Connell afterwards and told him what had happened, and he promised me he would explain it all to The Toad.

"Sorry, Annie," he said. "Mr Clarke must have got the wrong end of the stick. Don't worry. I'll put him right.

Leave it with me. Don't worry, I know it wasn't your fault."

Yeah, right, great.

Heart-shaped things that could be banned to make schools less threatening places for boys

Earrings and jewellery of all kinds

Bags and purses

Pencil cases

Notebooks

Cards

Buttons

Polka dots

Cakes and biscuits

Plates and dishes

Things that do not normally come in heart shapes but might be invented, possibly to fill the gaps left by the above-mentioned prohibited items

Scrubbing brushes

Saucepans

Rugs

Footballs

Tables

Laptops

Buses

Interactive whiteboards

Desks

Birthmarks

Shoes (!) – Maybe people's feet would eventually evolve to fit into them, and heart-shaped feet might turn out to be more stable than foot-shaped feet. A whole new species: *Homo sapiens corpedes*. You would have to redesign bicycle pedals and escalators and all kinds of things. Well, maybe not escalators, but probably weighing scales.

Chapter 8

Mr Softie

I used to be a light-hearted kind of girl. You could imagine my heart hanging out of a little parachute, or maybe bobbing along like a helium balloon, all smiley and happy. When I was young, like. Young*er*, I mean. Before all this. Before Jonathan went sailing out of my life, for a start.

"I don't doubt you, Annie," said Dr Thing.

He can be very encouraging. In his way. I suppose he can tell that I am naturally light-hearted. It's just bloody old *stuff* that is weighing me down. The things that happen to a girl, no matter how light-hearted she is planning on being.

"And now?" he asked.

"Well . . ." I said.

I mean, how *could* I be light-hearted now that all hell had broken loose? He should know that, I thought.

But I didn't say that. Instead, I looked out of the window. There is nothing to see out of his window. It is as if the interior decorator with the beige fixation had had a go at the exterior as well. There's a carpark. Is there a view more depressing than the view onto a carpark? Maybe people who are into cars might like it, I suppose, if there were interesting ones in it. But I can't tell one car from another, except I know a silver one from a black one. They are mostly silver and black. If I designed cars, they would be purple and yellow and bright green, like Skittles. The other things that should be all different colours is plugs. All the plugs in our house are black, except a few that are white, so when you are trying to unplug something, you have to try them all in turn, and you end up interrupting the dishwasher or one of those grumpy appliances that goes into a tizz when you unplug it and you lose all your data or your spin cycle or whatever. If they were all colours, then you'd know which one to unplug, and life would be easier. It's because men design stuff, and half of them are colour-blind. (It's true, it's some chromosome thing. Emma told me that.)

I didn't say any of this to Dr Thing, on account of him being a man. Instead I told him about this boy I think I am in love with. I didn't tell him who it was, that part doesn't matter, none of his business, but I thought it might do me good to talk about this love thing to someone who is not Emma. Not that I have a problem with Emma, it's just that she wants me to *do* stuff, find out where I stand, and look where that got me: Heartbreak Hotel.

Because I did ring Jono in the end, after that Keith stuff. I was feeling very low. I decided that Emma was right. She usually is. She is what people call a rock of sense. It wasn't because I wanted to know "where I stood", though. It was more because of the Keith incident. I don't know if I was actually planning on *telling* Jonathan all about the whole Keith thing, but it had unsettled me, and I just thought I'd feel better if I could talk to Jono.

I tried rehearsing what I was going to say to him, but no matter what I thought I might say, it sounded pathetic. What I really wanted to say was, "I miss you," but that sounded stupid as well as pathetic, so I decided I wouldn't say it unless it felt right. Which I knew, before I even scrolled to his number, it wouldn't. But if I was planning to say something stupid, then I'd never make the call, and I needed to speak to him. I needed to hear his voice. My heart had expanded so that it filled my whole chest, or so it seemed, maybe it was my lungs. It is funny how if you feel something in your heart, it is all romantic, but if it is your lungs, then that is just a medical thing, like asthma.

Internal organs in descending order of being OK to talk about

1 Heart
2 Brain
3 Stomach
4 Lungs
5 Liver
6 Womb
7 Kidneys
8 Intestines

Spleen and pancreas don't count, because people don't even know they are there, unless they have diabetes.

This was all just distraction therapy, I knew. I had to stop thinking about insides of bodies and actually make that phone call, but it is hard to stop thinking about your heart when it is banging off the inside of your chest and you think it is going to stop you breathing.

He didn't bloody *answer.*

And now I was worse off than before. Oh, God. Before, I still had the *prospect* of ringing him, something in reserve, something I could do if the worst came to the worst. The worst *had* come to the worst, or so I thought, and I'd blown that possibility.

Which meant, in effect, that the worst had got even worse. This always happens to me. I don't know why. It's not as though I am a bad person (at least I don't think I am, no worse than the next person), it's more that I seem to attract the bad stuff. This is tough on a girl, you have to admit.

Sometimes I wish I wasn't me, but then on the other hand, there is no one else I can imagine wanting to be either. Like I say, everyone has their own hell, so where's the advantage in being someone else? What you have to do is learn to cope with your hell. I've worked that much out.

Anyway, the alternative to being me might be being dead, and I don't think I'm ready for that. Not yet.

That's something, anyway. I don't seem to have a death wish. That is definitely something to hang on to. Even though my life is not a picnic. By no means.

So I imagined Jono sitting there looking at my name on the screen and *deciding* not to answer, waiting for the ringing to stop. *Answer it!* I screamed inside my head. But he didn't. He just turned off the lamp in whatever room he was in, somewhere in the world, got in under his duvet, and went to sleep.

I went to bed after that and plugged my earphones in and I listened to Lady Gaga all night long. She is good and noisy, and that was what I needed, something to keep me awake, because I thought, if I go to sleep now with the thought in my head about him not answering the phone to me, I might never wake up. I don't mean I would die in the night, I am not stupid. I mean, it was as if the me who woke up in the morning wouldn't be the real me any more, so I didn't want to go to sleep.

But of course I did sleep anyway, and when I woke up, I was still me all right, and the bit that was hurting when I went to bed was hurting even worse.

"This is not the Keith boy you talked about before?" asked Dr Thing. "The one whose name you weren't going to tell me."

Oops.

"I told you," I said. "Keith's a creep. This one is different. We'll just call him J, if you don't mind."

I hoped he wouldn't remember that I'd let the name Jonathan slip before.

"Jay? Is he American?"

"Yeah," I lied. I don't usually tell lies. But I found it kind of liberating. I wouldn't tell lies about something important, but what does it matter where J is from?

"The thing about him is," I said – and it felt all luxurious to be able to talk about him like this to a stranger, sort of a stranger anyway – ". . . the real thing I love about him, is the way he thinks he is so tough, only he isn't. He's just a big softie."

Mr Softie, that's him.

"Do you remember the way that ice-cream van, Mr Softie, used to come around in the summer – did you have those when you were a kid, doctor?"

He didn't answer. I am not supposed to ask him stuff. But I was just checking if he was following me. Anyway, if he wasn't, it was his problem. I'd given him the opportunity to clarify.

He didn't have a pencil that day, so I couldn't tell when he found things interesting. Maybe one of his other patients had told him what a giveaway it is.

Right, well, the ice-cream van, it used to play this tinkly tune. That big picture of a cone on the side of the van, the ice cream all piled up like clouds and those squiggles of raspberry cordial on it, and the music burbling away, *plinkity-plink*.

It was so *enchanting*. I know it was only some tinny

old music box, but the way you would hear it from far off, at first just a kind of a whiffle on the air, and then it would start to become more audible, you'd catch the tune. You might be in the kitchen peeling spuds or out the back emptying something into the bin or doing some really yucky old thing, and suddenly it would come wafting over those horrible concrete roof tiles and in between the weathered pebbledash of the neighbours' houses, and it'd be like fairy music, like in that poem where the fairies steal the child, and you'd think you were going to float off to the ice-cream kingdom and live off delicious things – berries and reddest stolen cherries – and marry a prince, and even when you looked and saw how algae had streaked all green and slovenly down the back wall of the house and how you had a battered old colander or something in your hand with little damp clumps of tea bags and disintegrating paper hankies clinging to its sides, still you thought you might be princess material.

"Only in your case, prince material, of course, doctor," I said. "Though maybe you never thought like that."

He resisted answering again.

"Maybe you just thought, *Oh, hey, it's the ice-cream van, must touch my mum for a euro.* Or a pound it would have been when you were young, doctor, but an ice cream probably cost about two pence, right? That's what my dad is always saying anyway.'

Dr Thing gave a little grunt, but I think it was because he was trying not to smile. People of his age (Toads excluded) find me quite amusing sometimes. He is middling old.

That could be a big difference between boys and girls: maybe boys just want the ice cream, but we want the dream. Boys really are much more different from us than you'd realize from just looking. I mean, let's face it, girls rock. And boys . . . well, no offence. They probably have other gifts. And on the plus side, they seem to need a lot of TLC for some reason, and, luckily, girls are good at providing that. It is amazing how well the world is organized. In some ways.

"Very poetic," said Dr Thing, about the whole Mr Softie riff.

I suspected the man of sarcasm. I am sure that's not in the Shrinks' Code of Conduct. But I forgive him. He knows when I'm doing the distraction therapy stuff, and I suppose he thinks I am wasting his time. But I'm not. You can't keep just looking into this black abyss all the time, because if you did, you'd end up wanting to throw yourself in there. Even though you know you don't really want to go there, oh, no thank you, but there could be a kind of centrifugal effect, and you'd just be sucked down, without even meaning to. Like standing too close to a train when it comes into the station. They say you should stand back from the edge, because you can get whisked overboard, so to speak, onto the tracks, because of the suction or something. Half the suicides are probably accidents, really, people who have gone into a kind of dream, one of those reverie things, and don't know what they are doing. That is probably what they mean about the balance of their mind being … whatever it is. Destroyed? Disturbed, yes, I think it's disturbed.

Nine things I love about J

1. The way he doesn't mismatch his socks on purpose to be funky, but they never match anyway
2. The funeral he gave his goldfish, just to make Julie feel better (this happened about two years ago, when she was only little.)
3. He was related to the late legendary Lulu Fortycoats
4. The way his eyes crinkle when he laughs – shut up, I know that sucks, but I don't care
5. He is not on Facebook, so I have him all to myself (when he is around, I mean; now that he is not around, it might be an advantage if he were on FB, I suppose)
6. That glass pebble he found in the schoolyard and gave me because it magnifies your fingerprints
7. The story about the time he ran away with his grandfather on the bus

8 The way he never lets on he hates the clarinet
9 He doesn't like cars
10 I am not going to put a tenth one in because it looks so final and that's not how I feel at all

I mentioned Mr Softie to Emma afterwards. She knows everything, only not in a know-all kind of way, in an interesting kind of way, like she hoovers up the Internet every morning with her cornflakes, and she said that when they take food photographs for magazines or posters or, she supposed, for the sides of ice-cream vans, they don't use real ice cream or not even whipped cream, they use shaving foam. That is so disappointing. I don't want to think of Mr Softie's raspberry-trickled ice cream as shaving foam.

Emma said it was because the shaving foam looks better, but I think that's cheating. Maybe it's really because the ice cream would melt in the studio, under the lights, so that's why they can't use real ice cream. That is a nicer reason.

Chapter 9

The Bad Ass

Well, of course, the Keith story didn't end there, or the Toady Clarke story, I suppose it had turned into by then.

When he got home that evening, Dad called me into the sitting room, and he had this look like thunder on his face. I never get into trouble with Dad. We get on really well. But that evening, he was out for my blood, or so it seemed. Something was up. Dad and I do not normally relate to each other in clichés. Expressions such as "a face like thunder" or "out for my blood" just don't come into it between us. Usually. So I knew I was in for something major.

I told Dr Thing all about this, but of course that was later. This all happened back then, I'm just telling it now. If you follow me.

"I had a phone call from your school," Dad began.

My heart stopped. Toad of Toad Hall. What on earth had he said to Dad that made him look like this? I hadn't done anything.

"Are you in some sort of *relationship*?" He said the last word as if it meant *toilet bowl*.

"No," I said. But I blushed. I couldn't help it.

I knew this had to be about the Butler thing, but what had they said to Dad?

"Are you telling the truth?" he said. "You don't look as if you are."

How are you supposed to look as if you are telling the truth? Not blushing, maybe? But I only blushed more. It was the *thought* of blushing that made me blush.

"Yes."

"Well, do you – eh – *fancy* someone, then?" And I swear to God, he blushed too.

"Dad, I am fourteen."

"So?" (Which is the kind of thing people my age say, you don't expect your dad to say it.)

"All fourteen-year-olds fancy *someone*, Dad. There would be something wrong with them if they didn't."

"Hmm," he said. "Is that so? I was under the impression that I sent you to school to learn your lessons, not to be horse-playing about with boys."

I let the horse-playing bit go. He was under stress.

"Dad, you were fourteen. You must remember."

"This is not about me, Annie. It is about you and – eh – inappropriate behaviour in school. With a boy."

Inappropriate behaviour. Clarkespeak.

I blushed again. All over. Even my knees felt hot.

"That's not true," I said. "At least, there *was* inappropriate behaviour, but it wasn't me, it was him."

"It takes two to tango, Annie," he said.

"It does *not*!"

My dad is cool and all that, but he is not so great on having a daughter who is growing up. He doesn't even like it if I borrow Emma's hair straighteners, that's way too grown-up lady for him. If he heard someone was trying to sexually assault me, he'd probably think I was all for it. He liked it better when he had a little girl that he can take to the zoo and the movies and the Bad Ass Café for pizza and ice cream. Which I am still all on for, pizza and ice cream is just fine by me, but he doesn't do that any more, maybe he thinks I am too sophisticated, which of course I so am.

"Who is this boy?"

"The one I fancy? Or the one I was . . . *tangoing* with?"

"The latter."

He always uses these solicitory words when he is angry. He is not a solicitor, he is a fitter with the gas company, but he is good with words.

"Keith Butler."

"Is he one of the Butlers?"

"Obviously."

"Well, I want you to have nothing more to do with him, do you hear me?"

"Yes," I said. "Good."

"What is that supposed to mean?"

"It means, *good*. I'll tell him, the next time he tries to *assault* me, that my father says I am not allowed to have anything more to do with him, and that'll definitely frighten him off I'd say. Thanks for the support, Dad."

I ran out of the sitting room. I had to, because if I had stayed a moment longer, I would probably have told Dad that I wished I had a mam instead of a dad, and that would have been awful. (As well as not being true, though I hardly dare to say that, because it makes it seem as if I don't care about my mam not being around. Which I do. More than you might think.)

A mother would have come in dead handy in this situation, actually, about Keith Butler, I mean, because there are things you just can't tell your dad. They are very touchy about their daughters, men. Get all worked up at even the thought of a boyfriend, not to mention unwelcome … *advances* (eeeek).

I stomped up the stairs angrily and banged my bedroom

door shut. I flung myself onto my bed, all set for a weep. Once I got going, I really did have a good cry. I cried long, sucking sobs and real hot tears.

I hung right across and over the edge of the bed, so that my hair was sweeping the floor and the blood all rushed to my head, and I had a good long wail for myself.

"Mammy," I moaned softly, like a little girl. "I want my maaaam."

Dad came and knocked on my door after a while. I'd stopped crying by then and was blowing my nose.

He said he was sorry, he hadn't realized it had been like that with Keith, and would I like to go out for tea. Jamie was playing a match somewhere off down the country. Which made it cheaper to go out. And anyway he would probably get chips or something, so it was only fair.

By the way, I'd had this kind of embarrassing conversation with Jamie the previous day. I was trying to find out if he knew where Jono was, but without letting on about how I felt about Jono. I mean, Jamie knows we're mates, but I don't think it has ever crossed his mind that maybe I might have a more *developed* sort of interest in Jono. I didn't get far with that line of questioning. Boys are never a bit surprised when their friends don't phone them. They don't expect to be phoned, even though I know they do ring each other sometimes at least. I don't think I will ever understand boys.

I said could we go to the Bad Ass and Dad laughed and said yes, and so we did, and it was lovely. It was like being ten again. Which would not be lovely in all respects, but when it comes to going out for tea with your dad, it is perfectly fine. Quite possibly the ideal age, in fact.

We got one pizza between us, because I know Dad is not rich, and anyway half a pizza is plenty, and, more to the point, that meant we would have room for ice cream. We were on the ice cream with butterscotch sauce when he came out with this sort of gabbledy sentence.

"You know your mother loved you, Annie."

I dropped my spoon. It clattered onto the floor. This was not the sort of thing my dad says. Not even Dr Thing would say a thing like that, even if he thought it.

I hoped the noise of the spoon would be enough to shut him up, or at the very least give me a bit of cover for not answering. But not answering was a useless strategy, because that made it seem as if I hadn't heard, so he said it again. This time not so gabbledy. This time dead clear.

"Annie. I want you to know that your mother loved you."

"Oh, *Dad*," I hissed. I bent down and picked up the spoon. Not that I was going to use it after it had been on the floor, but for something to do.

This really was no place, I felt, for a little father-daughter heart-to-heart. Weird expression that, makes you think of people's hearts popping out of their chests and having a bit of a natter, all blood pumping everywhere on the floor, and these little heart-mouths, these ventricle thingies, opening and closing like red fish. Or lumps of liver. Oh, yuck.

There I go again. Distraction therapy.

"Look," he said, "about earlier. That was a conversation for a mother to have with a girl."

My cheeks were flaming. I didn't know where to look. I waved the spoon vaguely at him, as if that might shut him up.

"And I know it's hard for you."

Oh, God, it was getting *worse*. What could I do or say to make him stop?

"Yes," I said. "Yes. That's fine, though, thanks, Dad. I need a clean spoon."

He wasn't interested in my cutlery problem.

"I want you to remember . . ."

"My mother loved me, yeah, sure," I said. *She loved Jamie more.* But I didn't say that part out loud. (At least, I don't think I did.) 'So it's it all OK, then, I suppose? That explains everything, right?" Oh God. I am such a jerk, but I couldn't seem to stop myself.

Dad was grey in the face now. This was much worse than the two-to-tango conversation. But he seemed determined to battle on. I'd say he'd rehearsed it.

"It is not meant to be an explanation, Annie," he said. (Come to think of it, he couldn't have rehearsed that bit, because he couldn't have known that I would say that.)

On one level, I was mortified. I was twisted on the inside with the sheer embarrassment of it all, but at the same time, I was angry. Not with him. With her. For not being there. For leaving him to pick up the pieces. For leaving me and Jamie to cope as best we could. For making me feel so goddamn guilty. For not explaining anything. For doing what suited *her*.

And then he suddenly stopped. He waved at the waiter, and called, "Could we have a clean spoon, please?"

As if nothing had happened. As if he hadn't made this dramatic announcement like a father in an American TV programme.

When we got home, Dad said, "I am serious about young Butler, Annie. You don't want to get mixed up with that lot."

"This is true," I said. "I don't. I hate him."

"You're sure?"

"Da-ad, I told you, he jumped on me. How often do I have to say it to make you understand? It wasn't me, it was him. He's a . . ."

"Guttersnipe?" said Dad.

"That's it," I said. "And a lout." That was what Mr O had called him.

"A bowsie," Dad said. "A gurrier of the first order."

"A scumbag," I added.

Dad made a face at that one, and I kissed him on the nose and he kissed me on the nose, like we used to do when I was little, and we were friends again.

Poor old Dad. I could see it from his point of view. He didn't know about how Jono had gone missing and how that made the whole Keith thing so much more horrible than it was anyway. But I certainly wasn't going to tell him about that (come on, you don't tell *parents* this kind of stuff), so how was he to know?

I didn't tell Dr Thing any of that either. You have to be selective. I couldn't really be telling him my whole life story, could I? And anyway, since I'd made the phone call that Jono hadn't answered, my head was wrecked. I couldn't think straight. I mean, I could think straight enough to cope with the Dad thing, but if I actually sat in a room on my own and tried to think stuff through, it was all just this mad swirl of thoughts, all jumbled up together like clothes in a washing machine and it gave me a sick headache even to think them, much less to disentangle them.

But the main thought, like two pairs of jeans and a denim jacket in the wash making the whole things seem indigo blue, kept being Jono. Where the hell was he? Was Julie with him?? And did he like me even the smallest bit? Except he couldn't, because if he did, he'd ring me, wouldn't he? Though maybe he couldn't because maybe wherever he was, whatever was going on in his life . . . maybe that made it impossible for him to ring me, so maybe it wasn't because he didn't like me but because of . . . whatever. But what was the whatever? Or had I just made up the whatever as an excuse to explain him not getting in touch with me? Did he like me at all?

See what I mean? Round and round and round and getting nowhere except muddled.

Chapter 10

Death by Bananas (and Random Vegetables)

I went over to Emma's the next day after school. That was the day *after* the row with Dad that wasn't really a row, and the day *before* the world came to an end. It is like a cat, the world. If it has nine lives, though, I really don't want to be there for any more of its deaths. There have been at least three I've witnessed already and I'm only fourteen.

We were supposed to be practising a hard bit in the Elgar. He is a composer, but you call the music after the composer. At least, the head honcho does. He says, *Open your Elgars. Page two, bar twenty-five*, so obviously that is the music, not the composer personally, because in the first place, there is only one Elgar, and in the second place, he is dead, and in the third place, dead or alive, he is not in the room. (Though I suppose there might have been more than one Elgar, when you come to think of it. Everyone has a family, and mostly they have the same name as you, or they did in the past anyway. It is kind of comforting to think of famous people as having a mother and a father, Mr and Mrs Elgar, no doubt, and being all normal like everyone else. Mr and Mrs Shakespeare. That sounds weird. Mr and Mrs Christ. No, that's wrong. That was Mr and Mrs God, wasn't it? Or no, oh, it's very confusing. I think the modern thing is better, where everyone is all partners now and you can't count on people in the same family having the same name.) And fourthly, and this is really the clincher, Elgar does not have a page two, he has, or had, a nose and ten fingers and an unknown number of teeth and so on.

Oh, dear, I am being skittish now. That is Dad's word for it. I call it being philosophical, but he is probably right. I just get these ideas and I have to see where they go, that's all. That's allowed. Or at least it should be. In an ideal world. Which I realize this is not.

Anyway, we were supposed to be practising, but we pretty soon got diverted. (*The clarinets aren't paying attention!* the head honcho is always shouting. *The clarinets are* talking. By which he means me and Emma, not the actual clarinets. It's a bit like Elgar being the music, not the person.)

It is nice being around at Emma's. I like her mother, she is large and jolly, like a mother in a story book. I call her Mrs Duggan, though she tells me to call her Sarah, but I've known her since I was two and I can't change now.

We've all known each other for ever. Once when I was only a little kid, me and my brother Jamie were round at Jono's house, it was way back, before Julie was born. I'd say I was maybe about five or six, and we were playing Lego and there were pieces all over the hall and next thing Jono's mam came down the stairs without any shoes on and she stood on one of them. They are very hard-edged, right enough; it would hurt if you stood on a piece of Lego. But she gave this great yelp out of her and she started cursing us and it scared the living daylights out of me. She told me, and Jamie too, to get out of her house and never to darken her door again. I didn't either, or not for years anyway.

Emma's mother called us for our tea. She is dead nice, Mrs Duggan, as I think I said. That is to say, she is nice, but not dead. Very good combination, that. Tea was pancakes with sugar and lemons. It was Pancake Tuesday, apparently. I didn't even know that. That's where a mother would come in handy. They have that kind of information.

She gave us bananas for afters. *Afters*, after pancakes! Emma couldn't eat hers, so I said I would eat it for her.

She said, “You want to be careful. Too many bananas are poison.”

That is a mad idea. Too many bananas cannot possibly be poison. I told Emma I didn’t believe that.

“It’s true,” she said. (She is probably right. She knows everything.) ‘Bananas are full of potassium.”

“Potassium is good for you,” I said.

“Yes, but too much can kill you.”

“Come on, Emma,” I said. “You are not seriously trying to tell me you can die from eating bananas.”

“You can. From eating too many. You can get potassium poisoning.”

“Well, I don’t think *two* would count as too many.”

“Yeah,” she said. “But maybe ten. Or twenty. I don’t know how many is a lethal dose.”

“Who would want to eat twenty bananas?” I said.

“I dunno,” she said. “Maybe it would be a cool way to commit suicide.”

I went still, very still, just for a moment.

But then I laughed, because what was the point of saying, all stiff and censorious, like an adult, *There is no cool way to commit suicide, Emma.*

And anyway that wasn't something I wanted to talk about.

So instead I said, "Well, maybe if you were in a banana plantation."

"Yeah, and very depressed," Emma added, holding on to her sides she was laughing so much.

Not that depression is funny, of course, but the idea of being depressed in a banana plantation somehow *is* funny. It's funny what is funny.

Then I had another funny thought. Maybe you could *murder* someone with bananas. I don't know how you'd get them to eat them, though. You'd have to put a gun to their head, but if you had a gun, why would you bother with the bananas?

"Are you a boy in a girl's body, or what?" Emma asked, when I said that about the gun and the bananas.

"No," I said, "but listen, it could work. They would eat

the bananas because they wouldn't know that was going to kill them. They would think it was better than being shot. And then there would be no evidence, because all you'd have done was to tell them to eat the bananas. You can't murder someone by just talking to them, can you? It's a perfect crime. I think I will write a detective story with that plot. You are not to steal it on me."

"You are such a *weirdo*," said Emma.

That's Emma for you. That is why she is my friend and I love her to bits. Not because she called me a weirdo, *obviously*, but because we have such good laughs together. You need a good laugh now and again. Even if you are heartbroken. Or maybe especially if you are heartbroken.

"Your mother really is great," I said to Emma when we'd gone back to her room, meaning about the pancakes and the bananas and everything. "You're dead lucky."

I didn't really mean she was lucky to have a mother, but I think that is how she took me up, because she went all doe-eyed and she asked me if I wanted to talk about it. She pronounced "talk" like "tock", which is a dead giveaway, because it means the person has gone into American TV-speak.

"Tell me about her," she said. "Anything. You can say anything."

I wasn't sure she meant it in the sense that she was ready to listen, or whether she just meant she was extremely curious, but I kind of thought the extremely curious thing was more likely (because of the 'tock' bit), so I didn't answer her for a long time.

"She wasn't much of a cook," I said, all of a sudden, because that was what came into my head. (Well, food is important to me.) "Not like yours."

Emma shrugged modestly, as if having a pancake-making mother is slightly socially embarrassing when your best friend has no mother at all.

"She was quite good at cakes," I said, "now I come to think of it, but she was terrible at dinners."

You might imagine a kid would think that was a pretty good deal, that cakes are more important than dinners, but actually it's not true. You get very tired of horrible dinners, even if there are good cakes.

"She was a bit better than Dad, maybe, as a cook, I mean, but that is not really saying a whole lot."

"You're very hard on your father," Emma said.

That was so untrue, I didn't even bother to argue.

"I remember a lot of meat," I said, because suddenly I did.

I don't much like meat. I am not a vegetarian, but I don't like big wodges of meat all the same. And that is what we used to get. Chops. Horrible word. Chop your block off. And gravy, awful stuff.

"Once she gave me a raw potato," I said, as a memory came gushing back.

"*What?*" said Emma. "To eat, like?"

"Yes," I said. "Can you believe it? A raw potato! I cried about it." I was only small, I was allowed to cry then. "It was raw carrots I liked," I said, to explain why I'd cried. "I hate them cooked."

"Yeah," said Emma. "Me too. Very boring. But raw ones are good and crunchy. You can get vitamin A poisoning from too many carrots, did you know that? But I don't think that's fatal, like too many bananas. It only makes you go orange, like you have a fake tan."

"But this potato . . ."

"It made you *cry*?" Emma said, her eyebrows wriggling above the frames of her glasses.

(She is not short-sighted or anything. She just wears glasses sometimes as a fashion accessory. Can you imagine being so pretty that you could afford to wear glasses for *fun*? Some people have all the luck. Sigh.)

"Yes," I said. "No."

"Which is it?" she asked.

"I mean, I wasn't crying about the potato *itself*. I was crying . . . I was crying because my mother could think I would *like* a raw potato."

"I don't get it," said Emma.

"I thought your mother should listen to what you said you liked."

"Hmm," said Emma. Her eyebrows had settled down again. "Have you ever thought that maybe you were a teeny bit spoilt?"

"God, Emma, I was *seven* or something."

"OK, yeah," she said. "Point taken."

Though she had a point too, I suppose. I was the baby in our family, never had a younger brother or sister to be jealous of. Thought my mam belonged to me, I suppose, and it was a shock when I discovered I was not the absolute dead centre of her universe every minute of the day. That's really what I was crying about, I suppose.

"Anyway," I said, "she totally lost it when I cried about the potato. She sent me to my room, but that only made me bawl more, because now I was not just hurt and disappointed in my mother, now I hated her for not understanding what was wrong with me . . ."

"Hold it a minute," said Emma. "You've lost me. What *was* wrong with you, exactly?"

God almighty, talking to Emma can be like wading through treacle sometimes. Makes you appreciate Dr Thing and his pencil-twirling.

"What I was really crying about was . . . well, it was – don't laugh – that my mother didn't love me enough."

She didn't laugh. She said, "Ah, Annie. She only gave you a potato instead of a carrot. You're making a mountain out of a molehill."

I slumped back against the cushion I'd put between

me and Emma's bedroom wall.

"We've moved on from the potato, Emma," I said. "Now I was crying because she'd sent me to my room."

"Oh, right," she said not very convincingly. "You didn't like that."

"No," I said. "I didn't mind going to my room. What I minded was being punished."

Emma sighed.

"She was my mother," I said indignantly. "She was supposed to love me absolutely. But first she'd disappointed me – and then she'd punished me for being disappointed. I mean, how bad is that?"

"Yeah, sure," said Emma again. "Poor little old you."

I laughed. It was a bit ridiculous, I knew, but still, I could remember the hurt of it, I really could, like an ache in my stomach.

Poor little old me.

I could remember myself opening the wardrobe door, which had a mirror on the inside of it. I looked at myself crying. I looked terrible, my face like a boiled tomato, all snot and tears. I was pitiful. But nobody pitied me. I opened the bedroom door and gave a few really loud sobs, to make sure my mother could hear me. But she ignored me.

That made it worse than ever. Now I could add cruel indifference to my list of grievances.

"But you made it up later?" Emma said hopefully.

"NO!" I yelled. "No!"

I pulled the cushion from behind my back and I clutched it in front of me.

"Oh," said Emma. "That's bad'

"We didn't ever make it up. That's the *problem*, Emma."

"So it's not the row that was the problem, it was the not making it up?"

"Yes."

"But it was just a tiff, Ann."

"I know," I wailed. "That makes it worse, though. Because it was about nothing. All the more reason to make it up.

See, after that, I was really horrible to my mother." I pummelled the cushion. "Everything she asked me to do, I did the opposite. I wouldn't even do my homework."

Emma shrugged at that.

"No, the point is, Emma, I was good at school – I was a nerd from an early age – and I actually *liked* doing my homework, but I started doing badly – just to get back at her."

"How did that work?"

"She was proud of me for being smart at school. She liked to parade me in front of the aunts and the neighbours and everyone, saying I'd got an A for my essay or a hundred per cent in my spelling test. So I started failing."

"Because she gave you a raw potato, Annie, and sent you to your room?"

"No! No! Because she didn't care about what I liked. She didn't care if I was upset. She didn't . . ."

And then I was sobbing and sobbing and Emma was thumping me on the back and saying, "Come on, Annie, you're grand, you're grand, I'm sorry."

She thrust a packet of tissues under my nose and I shook one out to mop up my tears and she said again, "I'm sorry, I didn't mean to upset you."

"You didn't," I said. "It's not you, it's me. I'm a mess."

"You're not a mess, Annie. You're just . . . oh, God!"

She stuffed her fist into her mouth and started to shake and shake. I watched her, appalled, until I realized she wasn't crying – she was trying to choke back sobs of laughter.

Now it was my turn to thump her.

"What's the joke?" I demanded. "What's so *funny*?"

Her eyes bulged with suppressed laughter, but she shook her head vigorously.

"Tell me, Emma, tell me."

At last she took her fist out of her mouth and she said, between sobs of giggles, "I can't. It's in terrible taste."

"It can't be worse than the banana plantation."

"It is," she said. "It is."

"What is it?" I insisted.

She turned her head away from me, so she wouldn't have to look at me, and in a strangulated voice she said, "Poor little Orphan Annie!" and she collapsed in paroxysms of laughter again.

Well, yes, it was in terrible taste, and I didn't find it all that awfully amusing – and anyway, I'm only half an orphan. But I could see why she found it funny so I gave a little grin to show I didn't mind.

"You have to laugh," she said, turning back to look at me. "You do have to laugh, Annie."

You do. You do. Or you'd cry.

It would be good if you could deliberately unremember some things. Then, if a person died, for example, you could just have nice memories left, and then you would probably feel better. You wouldn't feel so guilty. You wouldn't have to think that maybe that's why they died, because of you and how mean you could be.

Text Message

That was the last day of my previous life, my ordinary, muddled, heartbroken life. Because the next day was the one where everything went hell-shaped. The very next day, after the pancakes and the bananas and the raw potato memory.

Keith Butler was the start of it.

He came swaggering up to me on the street, his head all swathed in this oversized hood, and he blocked my path. I mean, really, spread his arms and legs out, and the whole pavement was full of Butler, and I had to step down into the gutter to get by him, and I was just slipping along when he turns, his arms and legs still all spread out, like Jesus on the cross or something, and wraps his big long gorilla arms around me. I swear to God they go around my body twice. And I am not anorexic or anything, I'm an average kind of size, though maybe a bit on the tall side. It was like being in a straitjacket, like a poor little insect being all wrapped around with spider goo. I thought I was going to suffocate, my mouth and nose felt full of his stinking tracksuit, and his body hard inside it.

I knew I couldn't wriggle my way out of this bear hug, he was too strong for me, so I just went totally limp, like jelly. It was the only way I knew how to resist.

"Mr Clarke not too pleased with you, is he?" he hissed, right into my ear. "And how is your dad doing these days? Disappointed in you, is he?"

What could he possibly know about Dad?

"Damn you, Keith Butler," I said. "Blast you to hell!"

He started to laugh. "Where did you learn to curse?" he said. "Because you are crap at it."

He suddenly let me go, though, pushed me away from him, as if I were the one who had been molesting him, not the other way around. Probably he remembered all of a sudden what Mr O'Connell had said about sexual harassment, and thought better of being caught doing it on the public street. But he still stood squarely in front of me, so I couldn't get past him. Come to think of it, I could have turned around and gone back the way I had come, but I never thought of that at the time.

He had this smirk on his face, and he took this little pink mobile phone with Pocahontas or Cinderella or someone on it out of his pocket.

"It doesn't suit you," I said. "It's too macho for you."

I could see he didn't know how to react to that. He knew I was being smart at his expense, but I don't think he could work out exactly how I was getting at him.

"Have you heard of phone bullying?" he said.

"Phone bullying!" I couldn't help myself. I gave a bark of a laugh at that. Partly out of sheer relief. "Has someone been bullying your poor little pink phone, Keith?"

"Ha-ha, very funny, Miss Clarinet. No. Someone has been bullying my little sister. Somebody has sent her a very nasty text message."

"Why are you telling me this?" I asked. "What has it got to do with me?"

"I just thought you might be interested."

In his sister? I didn't think so. I didn't reply.

"See, the way it is, Annie, some plonker sent my little sister a very scruffy text message."

I'd got that the first time.

"Really not very nice at all. Manky."

I shrugged. I couldn't care less who sends what messages to anybody in the Butler family. Though I was kind of curious about how bad a text message had to be for Keith Butler to think it was manky.

"Someone who very helpfully signed his message with his initials. The stupid arse." He gave a hoarse laugh.

I raised my eyebrows.

"JK," said Keith with a leer. "Know anyone with those initials, Annie?"

I wasn't going to give him the satisfaction of blenching, or whatever you call it when the blood all disappears out of your face like a curtain going down, so I kept as cool as I could and I said, "I don't know a bully with those initials, no."

"I was just thinking, the guards would probably be interested in this," he said swinging the phone from the tips of his fingers. "It's evidence, like. They can trace the text back to the phone it came from."

Well, of course they can. Anyone can see where a message has come from, you don't have to be the police. Unless it's a private number of course, but who does that?

"Really?" I said disingenuously. "They can do that?"

He is stupid, Keith, but only moderately stupid. He picked up the sarcasm in my voice right enough.

"Not only the number, Annie. They can trace the actual phone. They can find out whose phone it is, and . . . they can tell *where* it is. That might be useful, mightn't it? If a person had gone missing, for example."

"Might it?" I said carelessly, though my heart was thumping away like an engine.

I knew what he was getting at. If it really was Jono who had sent this 'manky' text message to this hulk's kid sister, then the guards were going to be able to trace him and he was going to be in trouble.

Stop thumping, I said to my heart. *Get a grip*.

Because not only could I not imagine Jono sending an objectionable message to a child, but also I couldn't imagine Keith telling the guards about it. I would think the only time he has ever been in a *Garda* station, he was taken there in the back of a police car. I can't see him voluntarily popping in for a little chat about a text message. Even if it was one that might incriminate someone else.

Keith was thumbing the phone now, looking for the message, and then he read it out: "If you lay a hand on my sister, you little bitch, I will personally come and beat you till you are black and blue and your teeth rattle in your poxy little head. Scum yourself. I know where you live. JK"

My God! I have to say, I was pretty shook by that. That was downright nasty. But who says Jono sent it? There are other JKs in the world.

I said, "Your *little sister* got this message? Denise?"

I don't really know why I asked. I knew he'd just said it. I was playing for time to work it all out in my head. It was hard to take in.

Mind you, Keith's sister is horrible. She probably deserved it. One day I was going past the kiddies' school on my way to band practice and Julie was coming out with the other littlies – this was a week or two ago, before she and Jono disappeared off the face of the earth – and this Butler kid is roaring at her, in that sing-songy voice kids use, "Hey, Jooooly Foooooly, we know yer ma's . . ."

I didn't catch what her ma was supposed to be, because this cheer went up from the other brats, they were shouting and laughing and roaring and cackling their heads off, killed letting this Denise one know they thought she was the queen bee. Julie just hung her head so that her hair fell forward and kept kicking the ground.

I dunno, I'm just saying, I didn't like the look of it.

But even so, that was a terrible text to send any little kid, even the horrible Denise.

"Danielle," Keith said, and nodded. "Not Denise."

I knew it was one of those names.

"It threatens to beat her up," Keith was whining now, as if I needed to have the text message interpreted to me. "She is only eight. It calls her scum."

I was starting to feel almost sorry for him. He was only sticking up for his kid sister, after all.

"And it is signed JK," he pointed out again. "I don't think that's JK Rowling, you know."

He gave a big bellow of a laugh at his own wit, and any sympathy I had for him evaporated on the spot.

I found it very hard to believe that Jonathan had sent that message, but if he had, I hoped to God he'd thrown his phone in a bin. Or a river.

Come to think of it, maybe that is why I couldn't get him when I phoned him. Maybe he'd chucked his phone away so he couldn't be traced.

Keith's burst of laughter broke his concentration, and gave me the opportunity I had been watching out for to get away from him. He was smacking his knees at the good of it.

"I don't believe you," I said, squirming away from him.

Because why on earth would Jonathan *want* to send such a message to the Butler kid? What is Denise – I mean Danielle – Butler to him?

Next thing, who comes pounding along the path towards us only Jamie. He is my big brother, in case I haven't mentioned him before, though I think I have. He is Jono's best friend at school.

He comes bombing along, building up momentum, and Keith is standing there gawping at him, and next thing Jamie bullets right into Keith and Keith falls back with a smack on the pavement, and Jamie is all over him, he's hanging on to Keith's ears and banging his head off the pavement.

I had to kick him to make him stop. Jamie, I mean. I was afraid he was going to kill Keith. Or at least do him some serious brain damage (assuming he has a brain). These things happen very easily. You read about it in the paper and the next thing a lad is up in court for manslaughter or something.

It seems Jamie had been on his way home on the top deck of the bus – he told me all this later – and he'd looked down and seen Keith laying into me, so he'd hopped off at the next stop and made straight for us.

He's a good brother. I haven't said much about him before, because he doesn't really come into the whole story much, but I'll say it now. He is a good brother, as brothers go.

"Go home," Jamie hissed at me, as he sat on Keith's body, keeping him pinned to the pavement.

"I can't go home and leave you here with him," I argued. "He might kill you."

"I'm all right," Jamie said, though blood was streaming from his nose. "I'll just have a little chat with your friend here, sort out a few things with him, and I'll be home after you. Put the kettle on."

I hesitated.

"Or *you* might kill *him*," I added, which seemed more likely.

"Go on, Annie," he said. "Scoot."

I stuffed a scrunched-up tissue I'd found in my pocket at him, and I turned tail.

I didn't go home, though. I went to Jono's house.

Putting Things in Perspective

I absolutely needed to see Jonathan after that, find out what the hell was going on. I knew there was no point in phoning, I'd tried that already.

The obvious place to start was his house. See if he was there, and if so, why he was lying low. That is how I came to 'break in' and that is how I came to find Jono's mother stretched out on the sitting-room floor with a fly buzzing wildly at the window and then the blue lights and the police and my dad coming for me and Dr Thing . . .

Now I come to think of it, there might have been more than one fly, because there was an awful lot of buzzing . . .

One good thing about it all was that it kind of put things

in perspective, though I have to admit, that was one hell of a perspective-changer. But it meant that my not having heard from Jono for a few days was "only in the ha'penny place", as Lulu Fortycoats used to say, Jono's old gran. She was always on about the old money. She called euros 'shillings'. "Because they look like shillings and that's about all they're bloody worth." Which I haven't a clue about, because what on earth is a shilling worth? Damn all, which I suppose was her point. Anyway, "only in the ha'penny place" means very insignificant, hardly worth worrying about.

"Stop right there!" Emma shrieked. "Back up, back up."

Oh, yeah, Emma was there for this bit, I forgot to say. She'd heard I was off sick from school, and she'd called by with a thriller (I don't read thrillers), lemons to make a lemon-and-honey drink (for my supposed-to-be sore throat) and a bunch of big daisies (which were nice) and she was all agog. (Well, the story had come out, about Jono's mam, of course.)

And I mean, agog. Imagine this very pretty girl with lovely auburn hair and very elegant spectacles looking just divine with her arms full of daisies (where did she get those in February?), and now imagine that her mouth is hanging open, her eyebrows have shot so high up her forehead they are half way to the top of her skull and she has this 'OMG' expression on her face. That's Emma all agog, and insisting on hearing 'the Whole Thing, Annie . . . Everything. You need to tock.'

I didn't need to tock. I had Dr Thing for that. But Emma was a good friend. She deserved to hear the story. She'd put up with me moping about Jono for long enough. She needed to hear the bit where I heroically went in search of him – and landed right in the middle of someone else's hell.

This was a couple of days later, of course, though it felt more like months.

"Yes, I know you went to Jonathan's house. But what I want to know is, why, Annie? Oh, let me work it out. You were going to stride up to the front door and say, 'It's all over, Jono. I hear you've been phone-bullying.'"

(I'd just told her the bit about Keith and the nasty text.)

"Don't be stupid," I said. "I just wanted to . . . I needed to know, Emma. Where the hell was Jonathan, why had he disappeared, had he actually disappeared, or was he just lying low at home, or what?"

"And had he actually sent that message?"

"Well, yes, that too, though I couldn't believe that. Still can't."

"Tell me what the message said, Annie."

"Don't you want to hear how I found . . ."

"Yeah, but I know that bit already. Shocking. Terrible for you. You poor thing, you look awful, but that's the sore throat, you must have had an awful cold. Terrible for him too, of course. But this thing about the text – this is a clue, Annie."

"We aren't the Secret Seven, Emma," I said weakly. "And I haven't had a cold. I'm out sick because I'm . . ."

"What?"

"Traumatized," I said. "That must be it."

"Oh, right, yeah," said Emma. "You must be. But, listen, just tell me what the message said."

"I can't remember." I gave a little cough. My throat really was a bit sore still. "Something about her being scum. 'Scum yourself.' Yes, that's how it ended. 'Scum yourself.'"

"Annie!" she yelped. "That's not what a bully says in a text message. That's a *reply*."

"What do you mean? A reply to what?"

"To *another* text, you dolt. If you call someone scum, you just call them scum, right?"

"Well, I don't call people . . ."

"Oh, shut up, you nerd, and listen. If a theoretical someone is going to call someone else scum, they just call them scum – though I know you are far too mannerly and Middle Ages to do that, but listen, if someone called you scum, what would you say back to them?"

"Scum yourself," I said.

"Exactly. You only add on the 'yourself' part if you are throwing an insult *back*."

Oh, right. That made sense.

"What else did the message say?"

I thought for a moment.

"Something about knocking her poxy . . . wait, 'If you lay

a hand on my sister . . .' that's how it started."

"'*My* sister!'" Emma crowed.

"That makes no sense," I said, "because it was *Keith's* sister who got the text, not the sister of the person who sent it."

"Yes, but I keep saying, it's a reply. Right, what's Jono's sister called again? Oh, yes, Julie."

"What are you on about, Emma, what has Julie got to do with this?"

"Listen," said Emma, her eyes sparking. "Suppose that turd's sister Denise . . ."

"Danielle."

"Oh, right, Danielle. Well, suppose this little turdette, Danielle, is the phone bully. And suppose she sends a rotten text message to Julie."

I looked at her uncomprehendingly.

"And then suppose Jono sees the text the turdette has sent to Julie, and he is mad, really mad, so he snatches up the phone and he bangs off this reply, 'If you lay a hand on my sister . . .' meaning Julie, right, and so on, and then he rounds it off 'Scum yourself', so obviously this Denise, Danielle, whatever her bloody name is, had called Julie 'scum' in her text."

"You're making a lot of assumptions," I said.

"Not really. We know Danielle is a horrible bully, we've heard her yelling at Julie outside their school, right? We do not know that Danielle can read and write – that is a big assumption, true enough, but, hey, she goes to school. So. We know that someone with the initials JK has replied to a text to Danielle's phone. I'm right. You'll find I'm right. Because we both know that the wonderful and gorgeous Jonathan Kinahan would not in his right mind send a manky text to a kid, so the only explanation is that he is replying to another, equally manky text, he is warning her off, he's not the bully, Annie. He's only standing up to the bully."

She gave a satisfied little sigh. And of course she is right. She has to be. It is the only explanation that fits the facts.

But that's all it explains. It doesn't explain where the hell Jonathan is now, and where the hell Julie is, and how the hell they left their mother for dead. And, by the way (though of course they couldn't know this), for me to find.

"I think you should ring him," Emma said. "Jonathan, I mean."

By now it had become a reflex action with her. Every time Jono came up in conversation, Emma advised me to ring him.

"I did," I said listlessly.

"You rang him?"

"I just said so, didn't I?" I said defensively.

"When?" Emma demanded.

"I don't know. The night we had the pancakes, I think."

"And?" Emma was practically bursting out of her skin with excitement.

"No reply."

"Well, but did you try again?"

"Yes."

I had rung him a second time. I had to, didn't I, after I *found* . . .

"Annie! You are so secretive!"

"I'm not. I haven't seen you since is all."

"You could've texted. Anyway, did he reply the second time?"

"No-o!" I wailed.

"Oh, Annie, I'm sorry. But maybe you should try again."

"Why should I?" I felt as peevish as I sounded.

"Well . . . possibly, just possibly, because you want to talk to him? You do want to talk to him, Annie, don't you?"

It is kind of amusing really, the way Emma is still so focused on how Jono and I should be getting together. I mean, in the middle of all this hellishness. But as I say, that is what is so great about Emma. She has this amazing ability to concentrate on the love interest in any story. Also, she is 'between boyfriends' at the moment, which is why she had so much head space to devote to me and my so-called boyfriend problems.

"Of course I want to talk to him," I said.

"I hope you're not going to give me that Middle Ages stuff again," she said.

I was beyond all that, though. I didn't care about who rang whom at this stage. I desperately wanted to hear his voice – but if he didn't want to answer me, what was the point?

I lay back on my pillows – well, no, I wasn't actually in bed, my cushions, then – and closed my eyes. I really couldn't take any more of Emma's enthusiasm for making phone calls. My life had moved on from all that.

"OK, Annie," she warbled. "I get the message. You're tired. I'll see myself out." She stood up and went to the door. "Oh, hello, Guard."

I opened my eyes. A guard. Another bloody guard! I thought I'd finished with the police after Dad came and picked me up from the *Garda* station that day.

What did they want with me again? They couldn't have heard about that text, they couldn't. I certainly wasn't going to tell them, incriminate Jonathan. I blinked.

It wasn't "they", though. It was only one guard.

Emma would say that of course they were going to want

to talk to me again, for God's sake, I was a witness or something and not to be such a wuss, it didn't mean I was going to be arrested or anything – well, I knew that, I am not stupid – but all the same, you do feel a bit wobbly when you find the police want to interview you – again.

Oh, God. Am I ever going to have a nice normal life?

She said I could have Dad with me. I would have preferred Dr Thing, actually, but I couldn't very well ask him, and also I couldn't very well tell Dad I didn't want him there either, so I went along with it. In the end I was glad it was Dad I had with me, because Dr Thing would have been twirling his pencil and driving me mad and he'd have found things out too that I'd rather he didn't know. This way, Dad found out things I'd rather he didn't know.

The things I'd rather Dad didn't know are different from the things I'd rather Dr Thing didn't know. If I made a Venn diagram of who knows what in this whole thing, I'd be aiming to keep the intersections as narrow as possible. Not because I am an especially secretive person or anything, but a girl has to be able to keep at least some of her *thoughts* private.

She started by asking me about why I "broke in". I keep

explaining to people I wasn't "breaking in", I just couldn't get in, and I needed to get in and the window was open so I came in it. I didn't break anything.

"But you climbed up on the shed roof," said the policewoman, as if that was a crime in itself. Which maybe it is, trespass or something, but it's hardly some desperately serious thing. Considering.

"To get to the window, yes," I said, as patiently as I could.

"And in your book, that's normal?" she asked with a little grin to show it wasn't a threatening question, though it was, really.

"Of course it isn't normal," I said. "But the only open window was upstairs and I needed to get in."

I'd already told her about how desperately I needed to go to the bathroom. And it isn't the kind of place where there are a lot of alternatives like public loos or a nice friendly hotel or anything. I could see she didn't really buy that. I don't know why. People do have to go to the bathroom. I know it isn't mentioned much in polite society, but it is a very strong motivator if you happen to be caught short like that. It probably explains far more things that happen in life than people ever admit.

She didn't argue with me about how badly I needed to pee, but I could see she really wasn't impressed with this as an explanation. It is very annoying when a person doesn't believe you when you are telling the truth. It's not great fun either when you are lying through your teeth, but it is especially annoying when you are telling the truth. Though I suppose there was a little bit more to it than I said (as in, I did also need to know what the hell was going on, whether or not Jonathan was there), but not much more, and anyway that's my love life, none of her business.

"About the blanket, Annie," she said.

I jerked upright on my sofa.

"What?" I said. "What blanket?"

"Did you put a blanket over her?" the guard asked gently.

Did I put . . . ? I thought for a moment.

I did seem to remember something about a blanket. It was so hot.

"I was afraid she might get cold," I said at last.

"So you put a blanket over her?"

I thought some more. I could see myself doing it. I could feel the cold coming off the body, and I could see myself shaking out a blanket and putting it over her. But it didn't feel like me, it felt like someone else. All the same, I *could* remember doing it.

"I think so," I said.

"Think some more, Annie. Are you sure?"

I thought some more.

Then I nodded. I could definitely remember tucking the blanket around.

"Yes," I said. "Yes, I put a blanket over her."

"When was this?"

When *was* this? It felt like something that had happened in a dream.

I shook my head.

"I don't remember that," I said.

Dad patted the back of my hand encouragingly.

The guard said, "That's OK, Annie. But you do remember . . ."

"Yes," I said shortly. "I do remember putting the blanket over her. I just can't say when, exactly."

She nodded.

Then she asked me the question I had been dreading.

"And what about Jonathan, Annie?"

I could hear my dad sitting up straighter on his chair.

"Yes?" I said calmly, though my heart was racing all over my body, tripping over itself.

"He wasn't with you?"

"*What?*" I said. I was genuinely taken aback by that one. "No. Of course he wasn't. Otherwise . . ."

I didn't finish that sentence. I thought I'd let her draw her own conclusions. She seemed to think she was good at that.

She was, actually.

"Otherwise, you wouldn't have needed to break in. Right. But if he wasn't with you, where was he?"

"I haven't a clue."

My heart began to slow down. It is a great relief to be able to answer honestly that you don't know something. I never thought I would be glad not to know where he was, but at that moment, I was supremely happy that I didn't know.

"Is he your . . ."

"Boyfriend?" I jumped in. "No."

Dad's chair creaked again.

"*Friend*, I was going to say," said the policewoman softly.

"Oh!" I said.

I felt as if I'd given something away there. Not clever.

"Yes, we're good mates. We were in preschool together, we go back a long way. His grandmother was a friend of our family."

I looked at Dad and smiled. He was very fond of Lulu Fortycoats.

"His grandmother?" said the guard.

"Yes. Mrs Kinahan."

"Not his mother?"

"No," I said, feeling my heart settling right back to its normal speed. I love telling the truth. It is so restful. "Lulu Fortycoats we called her."

"Did you know his mother at all?" she asked.

"Yes, of course," I said. "We've been neighbours all our lives."

"And the little girl?"

"Yes," I said. "Everyone knows Julie. She is . . . a little dote, you know."

"She's missing," said the guard.

"Yes," I said.

"We are very anxious for her safety."

"But she's with Jono," I said.

Oops.

“How do you know that? Have you been speaking to him? Or her?”

“No,” I said. True again. Thank God. “I just mean, it stands to reason . . .”

Which it did. They are both missing. At the same time. It is hardly a coincidence.

The guard said nothing for a while. I looked at Dad and he gave me a vague smile.

“There’s nothing more you wish to tell us, Annie?” she asked after a moment. “I mean, there is nothing more you can tell us that might be helpful?”

I knotted my brow, pretending to be racking my brains.

I was very tempted to tell her about Keith. Perfect opportunity to shop the creep and land him in trouble. But I couldn’t do it, because if I did, the story about the text message would come out, and Jonathan would be in even bigger trouble than he was in already. I couldn’t be sure Keith hadn’t already told the police about that, but in case he hadn’t, I thought I’d better sing dumb. It’s not as though it was *evidence* or anything.

"We are very concerned about Julie," the guard was saying now to my dad. "If either of you remembers anything at all . . ."

My dad nodded and said, "Of course, of course."

I don't know why they are all so worried about Julie. She is obviously with Jono, and Jono will look out for her.

And then it suddenly struck me. My God! Jonathan is a *suspect*. That's why they are afraid for Julie. They think he is some sort of a . . . They think . . . they must think, maybe they think he hit his mother, pushed her, *killed* her . . .

No! That's mad.

I had to ask. I couldn't not.

"Guard," I said, "you don't . . . you couldn't . . . I mean, who could possibly think . . ."

She looked at me with a blank expression, as if she didn't know what I was trying to ask. I suppose they train them to do that. I could see she was going to fob me off with some officious kind of an answer, so I went plunging on before she could say it.

"I mean, you aren't investigating . . . It's just about Jono and Julie being missing. It's not . . ."

She shut her notebook and said, "Thank you, Annie. You have been very helpful."

"But, what about . . . ?" I could hear the panic rising in my voice now. "I mean, you can't really think Jonathan had anything to do with . . ."

She smiled.

I wanted to punch her.

"We are just asking a few questions, Annie," she said. "We just need to establish the facts."

I put my face in my hands. It is all a horrible mess. I wish I had never been born. Or maybe I wish I had been born somebody else. If I had been born Emma, for example, none of this would be happening to me. Also, I would have lovely hair, like a tree in autumn, instead of like a straggly creeper in winter.

There, I am a superficial person. I found someone dead and a little kid is missing and a horrible text message has been sent to this other kids phone and God knows what is going on in Jono's life, and I am thinking about how

Emma has nicer hair than me.

But it is true. Life is not fair.

And Jono *didn't.* He *wouldn't.* He is *not* violent. He's such a teddy bear. (Only thin.)

Isn't he?

Chapter 13

Starfish

My mother used to think I needed toughening up. When I was small, I mean. She was always trying to get me to do things I didn't like. She wasn't cruel, that's not what I mean. But she must have thought I was a bit of a drip or something, and needed to be pushed to face things.

"Have a bit of backbone," she would say to me. At the time, I thought she must be right, that I lacked this backbone thing. I was like a jellyfish or an octopus or a sea anemone, just wafting in the current, and so I deserved no better. That's what I thought then, anyway.

I don't really think that any more. At least, I don't think I think it. Maybe I've grown out of it, that could be it. But these things do stick in your head. And in your dreams.

And in your dreams. Yes! That was where the underwater

dream came from. Hah! I felt I was getting places now, making progress.

I have this memory of myself in a bathing costume, one of those little-girl swimsuits with the skirts. It'd be like an ordinary body suit, but around the waist would be this deep frill, like a little skirt. It was a mad design, dead anti-aerodynamic, I'd say, but I think the idea of the little skirt was so that you didn't feel so naked, in case you were the kind of little girl who gets all embarrassed because she is in a swimsuit. Which possibly I was, I don't remember. It was blue with polka dots and there was white piping all around the hem of the skirty bit, like a sailor's collar. I used to walk into the sea up to my knees, and then up to the bottom of the skirt, and then a bit more, so that the skirty part billowed out, like a swimming-ring, so that you felt all buoyed up, though really you weren't, it was only a piece of cloth, and that gave you confidence and you could join your hands like you were going to pray, only you were just going to plunge.

And then this day, before I got to the plunge, this enormous pink jellyfish floated right past me, and then another one, and another, and I was surrounded by jellyfish and I was afraid to move, and I yelled for my mother, but she was swimming almost out of sight, all I could see was her white swimming cap and there I stood, shivering now, with my joined hands held out at chest level, and then I felt a jellyfish brush against my knee and I screamed and then I started to run but of course I couldn't run because I was up to my thighs in water, so I started flailing about, trying to keep my balance, but I fell anyway, down into the cold salty water, and I gulped a whole lungful of it, like awful cold snotty soup, and I spluttered and I couldn't breathe, and still there were jellyfish everywhere and I could feel their translucent eyes on me, their gelatinous bodies floating between the bits of me, and I was trying to scream and trying to breathe, and then my mother came and hauled me right out of the water, picked me up in both her arms. I must have looked like the heroine in a romance, my cold legs swinging over one arm and my wet salt-thickened hair drooping over the other, and me gulping and screaming still. I wasn't afraid of drowning or anything, I could swim, it was just that I was paralysed by being besieged by those wafty, transparent creatures.

"I was only *seven*," I said to Dr Thing. "Why should I have to 'have the backbone' to be able to confront adults and 'speak up'?"

That was one of the things she was always saying I should learn to do, my mother. Which is weird, because at the same time as they are constantly telling you to "speak up" and stand up for yourself, adults are also trying all the time to get you to shut your trap and give them a bit of peace. They really have no idea how confusing they make things for kids.

It's not that I'm blaming my mother or anything. It's just that this is the way things *are* between adults and kids. It's a condition of life, and the thing about growing up is, you just have to learn to negotiate it. But if your parent dies before you get to that point, it sets you back a bit. That's the problem.

I can remember that feeling, because it is not long since I was a little kid, but I suppose I will forget it when I get a bit older. I suppose I will probably turn into one of those irritating adults who keep telling kids to 'speak up' and 'shut up', practically in the same breath.

That is a depressing kind of a thought. I wonder if it's true, that nothing ever gets better, just goes on being more of the same, because people forget what it was like to be in the other person's situation, like adults forgetting what it is like to be a child. Maybe the whole world is like that, the whole of history. They say history repeats itself. That is probably what they mean.

Though I think maybe you could *decide* to change it. *I* could decide, for example. And maybe I will. I can try anyway.

I suppose that is one reason why it is a good idea to write things down, because then even if you forget them, you can check back on what you have written, or on what previous generations have written, or other people in other places, so then you have some idea what things are like that you are not actually experiencing at the time.

That was a BIG thought! Maybe I should study philosophy when I am older. I'd say that is the kind of thing you have to think about if you are a philosopher. I never could work it out before. I thought it was probably about whether there is a God or whether it is OK to kill that Chinaman where you can push a button and get a million euro and he is a horrible old man anyway and his family wants him dead. I don't know why he has to be Chinese. I think that's kind of racist, if you ask me, but maybe it's just so that you know it is a long way off.

I'd say it could do your head in, philosophy. But life does that anyway, so you wouldn't really be any worse off, would you? That's a cheering kind of thought, actually, though on the face of it, it might seem a bit gloomy. You have to look past the face of things. That's the trick with life. That's what I'm learning.

What Dr Thing said then was, "You're more a starfish, Annie. In my view. Not a jellyfish."

I'd kind of forgotten he was there.

He went up in my estimation, though. I know that's kind of sad, to be pleased if someone says you are a starfish. I wasn't getting my compliments quota, obviously.

"What is that supposed to mean?" I asked.

I was a bit suspicious of this idea, even though I was also stupidly flattered by it.

"A starfish has an exo-skeleton," he said.

I stared at him. "A *what*?"

"Exo-skeleton. Bones on the outside."

Oh, great, now I am some kind of invertebrate in a bloody *corset*. All the glow went out of the "star" part.

"Gee, thanks," I said.

"It's a good thing," he said. "An exo-skeleton. Most of the time. But sometimes it's good to let your defences down."

"Is it really?" I said sceptically.

"Really," he said.

He meant about the funeral, I'd say. But I didn't let on I knew that.

Instead, I said, "In sooth I know not why I am so sad." Which was stupid, because I have a pretty shrewd idea about it, but it just came into my head. "It wearies me; you say it wearies you." I'd learned that piece pretty good. I wasn't so sure about the next line, about "whereof 'tis born" and all, so I stopped while I was ahead.

"*The Merchant of Venice*," he said.

"Top marks," I muttered.

Which was a bit mean of me, because I hadn't been able to remember the name of it and he did, and he is *old*.

"School hasn't changed as much as I thought," he said, and he had this goofy grin on his face. It is amazing how delighted adults are if you mention Shakespeare. That is a good tip, by the way.

"But he's a bit of an old Eeyore, isn't he," he went on, "Antonio?"

I didn't know what that meant. I'd never heard of Eeyore. Though I Googled it afterwards and now I know what he meant.

"If I were you, I'd read Act Five," he said. "The love duet is the best part."

"What?" I said. I didn't think it was a musical, that play.

"It's near the end," he said. "Maybe you haven't got that far?"

I shook my head. We were only on Act One.

"'The moon shines bright,' he said. "Let me see . . . 'In such a night as this,' um, oh yes, 'In such a night as this, when the . . . sweet wind did gently kiss the trees, and they did make no noise . . .' something something something. Anyway, it's Lorenzo, he is sort of serenading . . . what's her name? It's known as the love duet."

He was starting to sound like Toad of Toad Hall, with his what's-her-name. But I mustn't let that irritate me. In every other way he is totally the opposite of Toad of Toad Hall, and you have to be grateful for small mercies, though this is quite a medium-sized mercy, I suppose.

I didn't know what her name was, in the play, the one Lorenzo was with. As I had just said, we haven't got that far.

"Sounds lovely," I said, partly to keep him sweet, partly because it did sound kinda cute.

"Are you in love, then, Annie?" he asked.

"Yeah," I said. "I told you that before."

He looked surprised. Or pretended to. I am not sure which. But he didn't ask me any more, which is just as well, because I wasn't in the mood for telling him anything about Jono just then.

What We Have in Common

There is something we have in common now, me and Jonathan. Only it's not like having the same birthday or the same number of brothers and sisters or liking the same kind of music and stuff. Those are the things you are supposed to have in common with someone if you are going to be good friends with them. Dead mothers isn't really the right kind of thing, is it?

Oh, God. My life, as I have observed before, is no picnic.

Nobody would tell me what Jono's mother had died of. It is very frustrating when people won't answer your questions. (I think I said that before too.) Dad said she probably fell down the stairs because she was sick or something. (For *sick*, read *drunk*.) Only of course she was nowhere near the stairs. Well, fell over a footstool, maybe. I didn't notice if there was one. Or it could have been a stroke, I suppose, or a heart attack.

Only there was the blanket. I kept coming back to the blanket, how it had got there. You do not put a blanket over yourself if you are dead. You probably don't even do that if you are stretched on the floor with concussion or a heart attack or whatever, even if you are not entirely dead yet.

But *I* had put the blanket over her, I suddenly remembered. Hadn't I?

In the end I did go to the funeral, even though I didn't want to, because Dad talked me into it. Sort of. See, what happened was, I was sitting at the kitchen table, crying my eyes out. I've started to do that lately. It suddenly comes over me, and I have to sit down and have a good old blub-fest. Only usually I do it in private; but this day it came over me in the kitchen, and I couldn't resist it (though I really am *sick* of crying) so I just plonked myself down at the table.

Dad came in and put a hand on my shoulder and said, "What's wrong, Annie, love?"

I couldn't think of an answer, because I didn't really know

what was wrong, so I said the first thing that came into my head, which was, "I miss Mrs Kinahan. Old Mrs Kinahan, I mean." Because I meant Jono's old gran, Lulu Fortycoats. Not his mother, who was an awful wagon.

I have no idea where that came out of. I did like old Lulu Fortycoats, she was a character, but it wasn't as though I would be *mourning* her or anything. She wasn't, like, family, she was just a nice old neighbour who used to make me laugh.

I thought Dad might give a little snigger or something, because I had said such a stupid thing, but he didn't. He sat down beside me, and he said, "So do I."

I looked at him, and my eyebrows must have been up under my hairline I was so astonished.

"After your mam . . ." he said, and then he stopped, as if he was waiting to see if I was going to start dropping cutlery and hissing at him to shut up, but I didn't, so he carried on. "After your mam died, Annie, she was so kind to me. She used to drop in with little flasks of soup and things, and she'd babysit so I could go out and get a walk or whatever. I don't know how I would have got through that first year without her."

"I don't remember her babysitting," I said.

"There is a lot you don't remember," he said.

I shot him a look, but I could see he wasn't being sharp, he was just saying how it was. They say you can repress memories if you have had a bad shock. I don't know if it is true.

I wasn't sure if I wanted him to stop, or if I wanted him to tell me more.

"And then that creep of a son of hers left his awful wife, and she just turned around and got on with helping to bring up those kids."

It took me a moment to process that. By "those kids" he meant Jonathan (*my* Jono), and Julie. And the "awful wife" was the woman I'd found stretched out with a blanket over her and a bluebottle buzzing up a storm behind the curtain.

I gave a little sniffle. He patted my shoulder, but he didn't say anything. I blew my nose and then I said, "Everyone I know *dies*, Dad."

"Ah no, Annie," he said. "That's an exaggeration."

"Death follows me around," I insisted. "Sometimes I think I nearly *make* it happen."

Which of course is stupid, but that is what it feels like. I have to say, my dad is great. He didn't try to jolly me out of it. He just spoke very reasonably and calmly and he said, "People do die, Annie."

"But I'm only fourteen and that's three people now."

"Mrs Kinahan – Lulu Fortycoats – she was ill, Annie, you knew that. Old and ill."

I didn't really know it, but it didn't come exactly as news to me, so I must have had some inkling, I suppose. I shrugged. OK, so she was old and she was sick. Not my fault, obviously. Fair enough. But . . .

"But then Jono's mother," I said. "I *found* her. It's . . . well, somehow it feels . . . it feels like . . ."

"What?" he said. "What did it feel like, Annie?"

"Like I just said," I muttered. "Which is stupid."

"What you feel is never stupid," he said. "Feelings aren't supposed to be rational. They're feelings."

"Death follows me around," I whispered again. "That's what it feels like. First Mam. Then her. And it's like I make it happen."

"That's not a feeling, though, Annie," he said. "That's just a twisted idea you have. You should try to think yourself out of it."

I could feel another snuffle coming on. I was so sick of all these tears, but I couldn't seem to stop them. How much water can there be in one head?

"Well, I don't know if it's a thought or a feeling, but I don't like it."

"It's pure coincidence, you know. You're just unlucky. You should go to the funeral, Annie," Dad said then. Whatever that had to do with anything.

"I *can't*," I said.

"It'll be better if you do," he said.

"You sound like Dr Thing," I said.

"Dr Who? Oh, right." He grinned. "Is that what you call him?"

"Better than Dr Who," I said.

"I'll tell you what," Dad said. "I have something for you. Something I have been keeping for you for when you are older. Something from your mother. It would be nice—"

"No!" I shouted. I felt panicky, all of a sudden. "I don't *want* . . ."

"Sshhh," he said. "Shush."

I was crying properly now, full-on tears and sobs, and rocking back and forth on my chair, and he was stroking my arm and saying, "Sshh, sshh, sshh," but not in a shut-up-and-pull-yourself-together kind of way, more in a there-there kind of way.

In the end, I stopped crying and I wiped up and I said I would go to the funeral. Because it occurred to me, they are hardly going to hold the funeral without Jonathan and Julie, now, are they, so this is my chance to see him, talk to him.

Jamie came too, which I was very glad of, and of course I was right: Jonathan and Julie were there.

It hadn't been that long, really, since I'd seen him, but it felt like for ever, because so much had gone on in the meantime. And, oh, I was *so glad* to see him. Even though it was a funeral, which, let's face it, is not my ideal date.

But it was even more terrible than I thought it was going

to be, and Julie looked like this very small ghost with a shadow on her face. The saddest part was seeing them coming down the aisle after the coffin. He looked so serious, and she looked . . . well, she looked like a little girl at her mother's funeral who really doesn't know what's going on. She was wearing these lovely new clothes, all in grey and pink, and she was admiring herself as she came tripping along, I could see her pointing her toes like an Irish dancer and looking at the pretty little buckles on her shoes. The daft daisy. She was doing the distraction therapy thing, like me, but she's only eight. (Like me, too.)

Jamie squeezed my arm as they went by. He's a good brother.

Seeing Jonathan – even just knowing for sure he was alive – made it very slightly less bad, and we hugged each other nearly to death only for the shortest time, and he said very fiercely into my ear that he would phone me soon, and then they were whisked away, the two of them, in this car, by a woman in a red coat and another short stout woman who looked like a duck in a dress.

And then it was all over, and the hearse drove off, he was whooshed away from me before I got a chance to speak to him properly, and there was so much to say, so many questions to ask, and it felt like the worst day of my life, except that it had this gold seam running through it, seeing

Jonathan for five minutes. And that hug. That delicious hug.

OK, so it was a funeral hug, the way you hug someone who has lost a person, it wasn't, like, a romantic hug, only it was that too, he held me so close, so tight, I nearly couldn't catch my breath, I knew it was more than just a funeral hug. And he kept saying, into my ear, "Oh, Annie, oh, Annie," and that wasn't a funeral thing either, that was an 'I love you too' kind of a thing. I think.

Of course he didn't phone me, though, after the funeral. So what else is new? But I am stronger now that I have seen him and know he is more or less OK, I don't mind so much. I do mind a bit – all right, *quite* a bit – and I am very curious, but at least I am not so worried any more, and so I suppose I can wait for a while and see.

That was a thing my mother was always saying, *Wait and see.* What's for dinner? *Wait and see.* Where are we going on our holidays? *Wait and see.* When will Dad be home? *Wait and see.* The answer to everything. And no answer at all.

Not that I blame her. She was just telling it like it is. We don't know. We never know. We have to just wait and see.

I'm still waiting.

Only I am waiting for her.

But I'll never see her again. Ever.

Oh, crap.

I don't know why she had to do this to me. It's not right. It's not fair. She's my mother, and she is supposed to look after me, and here I am and I have no one.

Except Dad, of course. Except Dad.

And Jamie. We're both half-orphans. Does that mean that together we make a full orphan? I must say that to Jamie. It'd make him laugh. And you have to laugh.

But it's not the same, is it? You can't tell me it's the same.

Chapter 15

This Woman

Dr Thing was dead pleased with me for going to the funeral. Dad too. It is weird how all these old men think that it is the *best* thing, going to funerals. Like eating your greens or reading improving literature. Maybe there is some kind of formula for living your life, things you can do to make everything OK and prevent death from stalking you. Something like this:

Recipe for a crushingly dull
but extremely healthful life

Spinach (fresh or frozen) three times a week
Bananas in moderation; ditto carrots
One mile brisk walk every day
Eight hours' sleep a night
Ten lines of Shakespeare every two weeks
Elgar, to taste (optional)

A good bracing funeral once every three months (or as the opportunity presents itself)

Yeah, great, and it is also better if you are not fourteen but about thirty-seven and able to imagine a nice bowl of spinach and a spot of Elgar as a cool way to spend a Saturday evening. (Though to tell the truth, I do actually like spinach. With nutmeg. And Elgar is growing on me. Maybe Emma is right that I am from the Middle Ages, or do I mean middle-aged? That is supposed to be terrible, but actually, all the middle-aged people – Dad, Mr O, Dr Thing, Mrs Duggan – seem fine, they are not going around fretting themselves to death about things, so maybe it's not so bad after all. When you get there, I mean. Not now. I don't want to be middle-aged just yet, thank you.)

Anyway, about a week or so after the funeral, this woman shows up.

Everything was just about getting back to normal. I'd even worked up the nerve to send Jonathan a couple of texts, not saying anything much, just keeping in touch, saying things like, *Hi, hope you're OK*, and stuff like that. Pretending I wasn't absolutely dying to see him, pretending to be just making casual contact, pretending not to care that he didn't answer, and all the time wishing, wishing . . . And not knowing if he even still had the same phone number, it was so long since I'd heard.

And then suddenly he started texting me again. It was *heaven.* I was *ecstatic.* Briefly.

She said her name was Kate, this woman, and that she was a friend of Jonathan's. And then I knew where I'd seen her before. She had been at the funeral, she was the woman who looked like a duck.

It was my dad who opened the door to her, which was lucky, because I wouldn't have known whether or not to let her in, but he must have thought she was OK, because he brought her into the sitting room and told Jamie to turn off the television and make a pot of tea.

It turned out she was Jono's social worker. I gave this big grin when I heard that. Just hearing his name does that to me, I can't help it, it's a reflex action, like when they tap your knee and you kick the doctor.

But then I thought, Oh, God, he has a *social worker.* Like a juvenile delinquent, I said to Dad afterwards, but he said that wasn't fair. (It was weird to hear him taking Jono's side. It's supposed to be me who does that.)

And then again, come to think of it, I have a head doctor. Is that better or worse than a social worker? It's all very confusing.

I was kind of interested to meet this Kate, since she seemed to know all about Jono, and I was trying to get her to talk about him without appearing to be all that interested, which is quite difficult.

But she got to the point pretty quickly. She said she had a message for me from Jonathan, and, naturally, that sent my heart into orbit. It started flying around in my chest like a satellite zipping around a very small sun.

"A message?" I said, trying to sound nonchalant, and probably failing utterly.

"It's about Julie," she said.

Julie! My satellite heart stopped orbiting. It did a nose-dive. He had a message for me – only it was about Julie. What on earth did Julie have to do with anything?

"Who's Julie?" Dad asked. Though he should have known.

"Jonathan's sister," said Kate. "Little girl, just eight. You know her, Annie?"

I nodded dumbly. My heart had sunk to my chest floor by now and settled down for a snooze.

"Jonathan asked me if I would ask you to do him a favour."

"What kind of a favour?" I asked warily. "Where is he anyway?"

I didn't feel all that like doing him a favour, actually. I hadn't seen or heard from him since his mother's funeral, apart from those few jokey texts, though he'd promised he would ring me.

Still, a message from Jonathan was a message from Jonathan. Gift horse kind of thing.

"He isn't able to see much of Julie at the moment," said Kate. "He's very fond of her, you know."

I nodded. She hadn't answered either of my questions. Typical adult behaviour.

"And he's concerned about her."

I nodded again. Still no information.

"So he was wondering if you would be so kind . . ."

"*What?*" I said. "What does he want?"

"He would love it, Annie, if you would go and see Julie."

"*Julie*!"

I didn't mean to shriek, but I must have, because Dad jumped.

Julie. What would I have to say to Julie Kinahan? She's eight years old.

What about me? Jono could have sent me his love, for God's sake, if he was sending me a message. That isn't exactly incriminating, people say that kind of thing all the time, it's not like it's a proposal or anything. He could have said, "Tell her I miss her." He could have said, "Tell her I'm sorry I haven't rung, but I will." There were a million little things he might have said. But no. He just said, "Ask her to go and see Julie." Like I am supposed to be some kind of remote-controlled babysitter?

"Sorry!" I muttered. "But I can't. Tell him I can't do that."

Nobody. Will. Ever. Love. Me.

I stood up and left the room. I didn't want anyone to see my face, because I am sure it had disappointment written all over it.

She reminds me of myself.

I couldn't face it.

Chapter 16

About-turn

First it was the funeral I wasn't going to go to. I hate funerals. That is not exactly unusual, I suppose. They are not meant to be enjoyable, funerals, are they? But I think maybe I hate them more than other people do. I mean, I wake up in the night thinking about funerals, with my flesh crawling and my teeth chattering.

Didn't want to be reminded. Didn't want to think of her under that lid with the crucifix on it. Didn't want to think of how Jono would be feeling. Didn't want to think of how Julie would be feeling. Didn't want anything to do with death and churches and organ music and hearses and people saying they are sorry for your trouble and all that *shit*.

But I went. I did it.

And now *this*. About Julie, I mean.

Dad said I didn't have to do it if I didn't want to, and I said I didn't want to and he didn't say anything more, and then, after a little while, he said, "I have something for you, Annie. I mentioned it before, remember?"

I shook my head.

He had put his hand inside his jacket and now he drew an envelope out and started opening it.

"No," I said. "Don't, Dad. Please don't."

"Annie," he said, "I think it's time."

"No!" I said, backing away.

"All right," he said with a sigh, and he tucked in the flap of the envelope and put it back in his pocket.

He looked very old, all of a sudden.

"Later maybe," I said in a whisper.

"You only have to ask," he said.

I nodded.

But I wasn't going to ask. I didn't want to hear. Why should *she* have the last word? Bad enough what she'd done, without my having to hear her reasons, her special pleading, her *case*. What about *me*? What about my case? Call me selfish, but come on, I was only *eight*. Or possibly nine. Young, anyway.

I wasn't exactly crying, but I could feel a prickling at the corners of my eyes all the same. I rubbed them and said, mostly just to change the subject, "Oh, give me that bloody woman's card." Kate's, I meant.

Dad's hand went back into his inside pocket and this time he drew out a small business card. He handed it to me without a word.

This Kate woman's name was printed on it on one side. On the other was an address in small, neat handwriting.

"That's where she's living?" I said, meaning Julie.

Dad shrugged. "I suppose so," he said. "Foster family, I think she said it was."

He was doing a very good impression of not giving a damn whether or not I went to see Julie, though I suspect he was secretly hoping I would. He probably thought it would 'do me good'. That is the way adults think. You can't fool me.

"Thanks," I said, and I put the card in the pocket of my jeans. I didn't say any more. I wasn't making any promises. I know how easily promises get broken, and I don't like that.

Suicide Notes and Jam

"*What?*" said Emma, when I filled her in on what had been going on in my wonderful life.

I think that must be her favourite word. She is always saying it.

"I told him to put the letter back in his pocket," I said breezily.

"Letter? Was it a letter?"

"OK, then, envelope," I said with a sigh. "I don't know, but in my experience, if there's an envelope, it usually contains a letter. So maybe it's a ticket to the circus or it's a gas bill or something, but I don't think so."

"So what kind of a letter do you think, then?"

Well, it was obviously a letter from my mother, but I couldn't bring myself to say that, so I just shrugged.

"Could be a *will*," Emma breathed. "Your mother's will?"

"Of course it's not a will," I said. "My mother didn't have any money. And we are not in a TV programme, Emma. In real life, ordinary girls do not get left castles or diamonds or the contents of Swiss bank accounts, and especially not by their mothers."

"OK, but her last wishes kind of thing," Emma said. "Advice to you about growing up, maybe?"

Emma loves a spot of melodrama: dying mother writes immortal words to soon-to-be-bereaved daughter.

But even Emma didn't suggest 'suicide note'. She mustn't know. Never heard the rumours. She was only young when it happened, of course, same as me. Though maybe it's just that she has had an unexpected fit of tact.

I shrugged, but I have to admit that later I tried to imagine what my mother might have written to me.

My dear Annie

You will be all grown up by the time Dad gives you this letter, and I hope you have had a good childhood and that now you are ready to make a good future for yourself. I am sorry not to have been around for you. I was never a good mother, too hard on you, I know you always thought. You're better off without me.

Still, I love you always,

Mammy

Probably not. Too coherent for someone in a state of despair. And you would have to be in despair, wouldn't you? (I hope so, because that is the only excuse I am prepared to entertain.)

Dear Annie

I can't explain it. But I want you to know, it's nothing to do with you. I want you to be a big brave girl and get on with your life now and always know that I love you, no matter what.

Love

Mam

Hmmm. That's her voice, right enough, but I don't think she'd go so far as to actually *write down* something quite so cynical.

Dear Annie

I know you must be hurting terribly, and I am sorry to be the reason for it, that makes me very sad. If I could not do this thing, I would not, but I can't help myself, it is all too much for me.

Your dad is the best in the world. He will help you and Jamie through this, and I know your lives will be better without me.

Your mother

WAY too sentimental. I'll give her that: she didn't do sentimental.

Dear Annie and Jamie

My dearest children, forgive me. I can't explain, I can only ask for your forgiveness.

Be good to your father. He loved you more than anything.

Best love always

Your mum

That was better. At least I'd thought to include Jamie, though he doesn't need a letter, because Jamie is fine, perfectly fine. It never occurs to him that he might have had anything to do with it, and he's right, because she was mad about him.

I'm so sorry Annie.

I like jam.

Mam

That's my favourite. If she wrote that, I'd forgive her, actually. I really would. It's the jam that does it!

You see, the thing is, when you remember, you have to remember the right things – that's the trick. I remembered the jam, and everything else just somehow clicked. My God, the relief! The jam! It actually made me smile.

But I should explain.

It was my mother who taught me how to read. I was sick for the longest time, and I missed a whole lot of school, and Mam thought I might be missing out on reading. I was only four. They don't teach you reading at four. But she didn't know that. So she bought all these reading books with five words on every page, dead boring, all about these awful kids with terrible hair throwing ball or playing with their stupid dogs and saying "Good dog". I was so bored, I learned to read them real fast, so she would buy me books with more words in them, where there might be a proper story. She did, but they were still boring. Even with more words, they were still saying very stupid things like "Well done, Jack" and "Thank you, Mummy" and "I like jam".

"We all like jam," I remember her saying. "We don't have to write a *book* about it."

That made me giggle, and she giggled too, and after that, we used to say 'I like jam' in this silly voice when we thought something was stupid.

There was one book with an elephant in it. That was better. She had a red dress, and she looked a lot like my teacher. And she never mentioned jam.

Anyway, that is how I learned to read, and when I had learned to read enough, then she taught me how to write. She bought me these old-fashioned copybooks with coloured lines and she showed me how to make the letters keep inside the lines.

That was more fun, because then I could write my own stories.

"We like to throw jam. Good ball. Dogs like jam. Elephants throw dogs. Do you like good elephants?"

She used to laugh at that. The two of us used to have these competitions to see who could make up the silliest sentences with the stupid words.

I have to admit that was nice, really nice. I will save it up to tell Dr Thing next time I see him. He likes it when I have 'positive memories'.

Men are easy. It's just struck me. Not always pleasant, but easy. Even Toady Clarke is easy. Sleazeball Butler too, once you get the hang of him.

Jonathan is the only one I find difficult. It must be a love thing.

Damn.

Like the song says, love hurts.

The jam is the thing, though. I have to just keep remembering about the jam.

Chapter 18

Mr O

I decided I would go back to school. I couldn't be sitting around at home moping all the time and crying at the kitchen table and writing suicide notes to myself. (How weird is *that*?)

Dr Thing thought it was a good idea. He didn't go so far as to say so, of course, but he gave this satisfied little nod. That nearly made me want to change my mind, but I didn't. (That would be just too sad, to be getting my kicks out of thwarting Dr Thing.)

The first person I met was Mr O'Connell. He doesn't teach our class. I wish he did, because he is the best teacher, in the sense of being the best *human being* who teaches in our school. Possibly he is a terrible *teacher*, though I doubt it.

"Ah, Annie," he said. "There you are. How are you?"

He is one of the few people who means it when they say 'How are you?' They actually want to know how you are. I smiled at him, because I like him, but I didn't want to say 'Grand, and yourself?' which is the polite answer. Nor did I feel up to telling him how I actually was. I didn't think he'd like to hear about the frondy nightmare, for example. Or the imaginary letters. So I just smiled.

"Saw you at the funeral," he said, lowering his voice.

I hadn't seen him, didn't realize he'd been there.

He caught me by the wrist. They are not supposed to touch us, teachers, which I can understand the reason for, but it makes things feel very eerie at times, like we are all cyborgs or something. So when he did that, it felt slightly weird, but in a good way. So I patted the back of his hand, as if I was the older person and he was the student, which he probably thought was a bit peculiar, but I wanted him to know it was all right that he had reached out like that.

"Tough on you, Annie," was all he said.

"Yeah," I said.

"If ever . . ." he said, and he tapped a finger lightly to his own breastbone.

I knew that meant I could talk to him if I wanted to. I didn't want to, so I shook my head, and the best part was that he nodded at that. I didn't have to want to. Mr O'Connell for president! Or for principal of our school, even better. Which will never happen, because the nicest teachers never get to be the boss. It's the ones who obsess about your socks or whether your ear-rings are regulation-compliant who get to be in charge.

"There's a little girl," he said.

"Yeah," I said. "Julie."

"Tough on her," he said.

Same thing he'd said about me. That jolted me. I don't know why it should have, but it did. It made the inside of my nose fizz. I nodded.

"Well, you know yourself," he said, and then he let go of my wrist and walked on.

I do know myself. I, myself, know.

That decided me. (Yes, I *am* a hero. I don't mind admitting that.)

The second person I met was Emma. She flung her arms

around me and whooped in my ear. I got the impression that she was glad I'd come back to school.

"I'm going to see Julie Kinahan," I told her.

She knew about that visit we'd had from the duck woman. Kate, but I'd told her I wasn't going to do it.

"Why on earth …?"

I didn't answer.

Instead, I just said, "She's in a foster family."

I took Kate's card out and showed it to Emma.

"Oooh-er," she said, reading the bit about the social worker on the front.

"The address on the back, that's where Julie is fostered."

"Does that mean she's been adopted?" asked Emma.

"No," I said. "I thought you knew everything. I looked it up on the internet. Fostering is what they call it when you are living in somebody's real house with parents who are not your own parents, instead of in a children's home, but you have not been adopted, it is maybe only a temporary arrangement, until your own parents are able to mind you again."

"Not very likely in Julie's case," said Emma. "Her dad doesn't want anything to do with her, I hear. And her mother . . ."

"Yes, well, ghosts do not make good parents," I said. "I can tell you that for nothing."

"Tough on her," said Emma, sounding very adult.

Yeah, yeah, well, I am doing what I can.

"Are you sure you want to do this?" Emma asked. "I mean, Julie is not your problem, Annie."

"She is Jono's problem, though."

"So? Jono's problems are not . . ."

"Look, Emma, I am doing this, OK?"

"OK," she said, physically backing away from me. I must have spoken more fiercely than I'd realized. "OK, keep your knickers on."

"Hair, you idiot. Knickers get in a twist. Hair gets kept on."

Chapter 19

Turdface Again

So there I was, after school, jogging along Julie's road, counting the houses – half of them had no numbers written up; it should be against the law, it makes it very difficult to find places if there are no numbers – when who the hell should I meet but Turdface Butler! I could hardly believe it. I'd nearly forgotten that that creep even existed. So much had happened in my head since I had last seen him.

I wanted to turn around and slink off home. I really didn't feel up to another confrontation with the scum of the earth. And then of course Jamie had had … eh … a few *words* with him. Was this going to make Keith even more aggressive, or was he going to look sheepish or what?

But I had decided I was going to see Julie – because that was what Jono had asked me to do, I was doing it for him – and if that meant I had to climb the Keith mountain to do it, well, OK. I'd survived the last encounter, lived to tell the tale, so I braced myself, lowered my eyes and kept moving.

He did his usual stunt of stepping right into my path so I couldn't get by, and he said, "Hello, Annie, how are you?"

Now, *that* was one of those fake 'How are you's' for sure, so I didn't bother to reply. I just stared at him, trying to look very bored.

"Haven't seen you since the funeral," he said.

The funeral? He'd been at Jono's mother's *funeral*?

I didn't respond.

"My ma wanted to go," he said, as if he'd read my mind. "I went with her."

He sounded nearly civilized. Possibly because of what Jamie did to him.

But I still said nothing. If I'd opened my mouth the wrong words would have come out. I would have said something nasty about his mother wanting to gloat, and there would have been no point in that: it might not even be true (I hardly knew his mother) and it certainly wasn't going to smooth my way with her horrible son.

Then he said, "What are you doing around here?"

"Same as you," I said, dead cool, like, "walking along on the public footpath, minding my own business."

I hoped he'd get the hint, that he was supposed to be minding his own business. But he's not good at picking up on hints, Keith. He doesn't do subtle.

"You're friendly with that Emma Duggan one, aren't you?" he said.

"*What?*"

"The one with the hair," he said, as if he thought maybe I didn't know who Emma was.

"And . . . eh . . . you know . . ." he added.

He made a curvy gesture in the air that had nothing whatsoever to do with hair and I swear to God his tongue protruded from the side of his mouth. Which proves that it is not congenitally attached to his hard palate, so he has no excuse for talking as if it is.

I shuddered. I have never been so glad to be on the

challenged side in the curves department. He really is a total slime ball.

"She is gorgeous. You have to admit. Hot."

I am relatively gorgeous myself, I like to think. Well, I have hair. OK, so it isn't a blaze of glory, but, hey, I am female, and young, and I have the right number of arms and legs and even if I do wear glasses, I have contacts for weekends. I am *presentable.* (Not that I think people without the right number of arms and legs are not presentable – I would hate anyone to think I am disabledist, but what I am trying to say is – oh, maybe I should just shut up.)

How come *Keith Butler* was making me have these defensive thoughts? He is a toe-rag. A total toe-rag. With athlete's foot.

I do have to do something about my hair, though. I really do.

"Yeah, but *you're* not," I said at last. It took me a while to make this riposte, but he'd taken me by surprise.

"Fellas don't have to be gorgeous," he said confidently.

"No?" I asked.

"No. Fellas just have to be fellas."

"I see," I said.

"Look, I know you fancy me something rotten," he said.

I wanted to kick him on the shins. No, I wanted to kick him a bit higher up, actually. I gritted my teeth.

"But, you know the way it is," he went on. "I just don't feel the same way about you, Annie. You and me, well, it looked like . . . but lately, I've been thinking, maybe not . . . after all, like."

That was quite a speech for Tongue-tied Butler. And it didn't even have the word 'hot' in it.

He gave this big ingratiating grin. It made him look like one of those meat-eating dinosaurs with the mouth that goes three-quarters way round their skull. *Shudder.*

I could feel this pressure in my nose, like a sneeze and a laugh all rolled up into one. I had to work hard to stop it coming out as a snort. He'd been *thinking.*

I wished I had twenty bananas and a loaded gun.

"Emma is spoken for," I said at last. Which was not true.

She owes me one. Big time. I must remember to tell her. Maybe she will give me those hair straighteners altogether, considering she is already so gorgeous that even Totally Toe-rag Butler could see it.

"What does that mean?"

"It means you haven't a hope," I said. "Listen, do you know where this person lives?"

I showed him the address I had in my hand. Normalizing of relations, you call that. Like after a war.

It seemed to work. He suddenly started talking and acting like a normal human being. I mean, you ask them a question and they do their best to give you the information you have asked them for. I don't know how I managed this transformation. I wish I did, so I could be ready with the magic behaviour next time I have an unwelcome encounter with a girl-eating monster.

"Our house is over there," he said, pointing.

"*Your* house!" I said, my heart in my mouth.

Holy God, they couldn't have given Julie to the *Butlers*, could they! *Could* they?

"Yeah," he said. "That's my little sister playing there on the scooter. Danielle. The one your friend Jonathan was trying to terrorize. Your fella, isn't he, Annie? The lad that's banged up in the juvenile."

"The juvenile?"

"Prison for kids," he explained.

My heart was beating in my ears now, and there was a pulsating band around my head, as if I was wearing some kind of headphone thing that was too tight. Way too tight.

"And that's the Walkers' house," he was saying, still pointing, as if he hadn't just driven a tank through my heart. "Next door."

Prison. My vision had gone all wavy, and my mouth was dry.

"Bloody Jean Walker takes in scum kids," he was saying. "Snotty bitch. Thinks we're all scobies around here, all except her with her French windows and her scum foster kids . . ."

I just walked away. I couldn't be bothered listening to him whining.

Prison rang in my head. *Prison*, in time with every step I took. How could they have put Jonathan in prison? *Prison*, *prison*. And for what? For running away? For abducting Julie?

But I couldn't think about that. I had to concentrate on where I was going. The green recycling bins were all out, waiting for collection, which made the place very congested. I had to thread my way between bicycles and scooters and kids and bins.

Keith Butler is *such* a turd. And my hair is perfectly all right. I think it is time natural waves came back.

You Don't Have to Be Frankenstein

The Butlers' house had one of those cobble-look drives and these flowery curtains in all the windows.

I checked with Danielle about where Julie lived.

"The one whose ma died?" she said, and she immediately cupped her hand to her mouth and made big eyes, as if she'd mentioned something unspeakable.

"That's right," I said, hoping my gritted teeth wouldn't be obvious in my voice.

"She was an alco," said Danielle, swinging her hair behind her head. This pronouncement didn't merit a hand-across-mouth gesture. It was OK to say that, apparently.

"Who?"

"Her *ma*," said Danielle contemptuously. "That died. Drank herself to death. That's what my ma says."

"Really?"

Lovely woman, her ma, evidently, I wanted to remark, but didn't.

"Yeah," said Danielle, warming to her theme. "They do that. They get out of it, don't know what they're at, and then, *wumph*, least thing takes them off. Flu. Or a fall."

She sounded like an old woman.

"Is that so?" I could feel the anger rising in me, but I kept telling myself, *She's only a kid, she is only repeating what she is hearing.*

"Yeah," she said. "We don't like alcos," she added.

"Do we not? And why is that?"

"They're . . . *drunks*," explained Danielle.

"And that's bad?"

I was talking to her across their recycling bin. It was bulging with bottles and cans. You aren't even supposed to put bottles in the recycling. You are supposed to take them to the bottle-bank outside the supermarket. And they hadn't flattened their cans either.

She looked a bit uncertain, but she nodded.

"And why would that be?" I asked. I was starting to enjoy this.

"They're spongers," she said.

"What's that?"

"They sponge up drink," she said. "Disgusting."

"Ah," I said. "I see."

"Whiskey," she whispered hoarsely. "And beer."

I looked pointedly at the beer cans in her family's bin, but she was too young (or possibly too stupid) to make the connection.

"Anyway, which house is Julie in?" I asked.

Danielle pointed. "Lives with bloody Jean."

"Thank you, Denise," I said.

"Danielle," she said, indignant.

"Ah, yeah," I said. "Knew it was a boy's name."

She went purple.

I knocked on Bloody Jean's door, and explained that I had come to see Julie.

Jean flung the door open and gave me a great big beam, as if she had been expecting me. But I showed her Kate's card anyway, so she'd know I was above board, though I don't think I look like a child molester or anything, but then I suppose child molesters don't look like child molesters, that's the trick, isn't it?

I had never been in a house like it. I mean, it was the same as all our houses, on the outside, but inside, it was totally different. They'd taken out the wall between the front room and the back room, made it all one big long room, very bright, with a wooden floor. The hall had a wooden floor too. The big room had a glass door at the end of it, which opened out into the garden, and on one side of the door were two little desks, with schoolbags on the chairs.

"Homework corner," said Jean, watching me looking. "They've finished, though, for today. They're in the garden now."

I followed her out the glass doors. Julie was pushing another girl on a swing, and they were both singing at the tops of their voices.

"Visitor for you, Julie."

Julie stopped pushing and looked at me. Her face was still a strange colour on one side. Kind of yellow ochre, as if she'd been messing about with stage make-up.

"You're Jono's girl!" she said, her face breaking into a smile. "But I forget your name."

I told her my name, and she came and took my hand.

"Of course," she said. "Annie. I knew that really."

"I thought *you* were Jono's girl," I said, as we sauntered back into the house.

"No," she said. "I'm his sister."

"I see."

She stopped and looked up at me. "You *knew* that!" she said accusingly.

"I thought that," I said. "What makes you think *I* am his girl?"

"Well, he has *three* photographs of you," she said, counting one, two, three on her fingers, as if I might not know how many that was.

I could feel this big goofy smile growing right across my face. I couldn't help it.

"And he writes your name all over everything. You don't have to be Frankenstein to work it out."

I stared at her.

"Oh!" I said, after a beat. "Einstein, you mean. You don't have to be Einstein to . . ."

"That's what I *said*," she said.

We were in the big room now, at the other end of it, sitting on a sofa. We could hear Danielle and her mates outside at the front, singing a skipping song.

"I hate her," Julie whispered to me, cocking her head in Danielle's direction. "She's a bully. But I told on her. She got into trouble over sending mean texts."

Scum yourself. Emma was right.

"They took her phone off her," Julie said. "But now she sends anomalous texts from other people's phones."

"If they're anonymous, Julie, how do you know they come from her?"

"Anomalous," Julie corrected me. "I know her words."

I put a finger to the yellow patch on her face.

"What happened?" I asked. "Was it Danielle?"

She shook her head.

"It's nice here," she said, looking around, "isn't it? Except that Jonathan isn't here. That's the problem."

Prison, I thought, and a lump formed in my throat.

"Your mam's dead, isn't she?" Julie said then. "Same as mine."

I nodded.

"That's sad," she said.

"Yeah," I muttered. I couldn't say any more. I was too choked up.

"I saw you at my mam's funeral," she said.

"Yeah," I said again.

"What did *your* mam die of?" she asked suddenly.

I froze. I don't talk about that. Not to anybody.

Julie looked at me, her face all creased with concern.

"Cancer?" she asked, in a dread whisper.

"No," I croaked, my hand at my throat. What was I going to tell this child?

"Heart attack?"

"No."

"Accident? Like mine?"

I shook my head.

"What, then?" she asked.

I said nothing for the longest time. My heart was twisting itself inside out. She seemed to be holding her breath.

"Sadness," I said in the end. I didn't want to lie to her. That was the closest I could come to the truth. (She's only eight.)

"Does that kill you?" Julie said softly, her head cocked on one side.

"In a way," I said.

"Oh, I see," she said, very matter-of-fact. "Tablets, then. Probably."

I gulped. My face wanted to crumple, but I wouldn't let it.

"Poor you," Julie said, in a strangled voice, and she flung her chubby little arms around my neck.

"Poor you, too," I said, burying my face in her hair and rocking her. She smelled of lemons.

Julie said then, "I love your hair." She is the *nicest* child. "It's dead shiny. Do you wash it in something special? Rainwater?"

"Just tap water," I said, "and shampoo. I was thinking of putting streaks in it."

"Oh, no!" she said, fingering a lock of it and letting it slip along her hand, catching the light. "It's lovely the way it is."

I could feel a tear trickling warmly down my face. I don't know where it came from. I don't feel *that* strongly about my hair.

Julie produced a tissue out of a box on the coffee table and handed it to me.

"It's not your fault," she said.

"*What?*" I asked. I was still on the hair theme.

"It's not your fault," she repeated. "About your mam. Jean says, it's never the little girl's fault, if the mammy dies. No matter what."

I said nothing to that, but I was thinking, *Yeah, right, and Jean knows everything.*

"She knows," Julie said, as if she could read my mind. "Jean. She has had *sixteen* foster-children. Imagine! Sixteen. They only take the tablets because they love you."

That was daft. No matter what Jean said.

Julie said, "It's because they are not thinking straight. They think they can't love you enough. That can't be your fault, can it?"

What is this kid, a psycho-what's-it? But I felt warm inside, all the same. Dr Thing'd love this. He could give Julie a job, cheering up the patients. Though maybe not. She might put him out of business.

"It could happen to a bishop," I said, remembering Lulu Fortycoats's phrase again.

"My *gramma* used to say that," Julie said with a delighted smile. And then, as if that reminded her, she asked, "Will you read me a story?"

"Can you not read yet?" I asked her.

"Yes," she said. "But I need another person for the voices."

"Right," I said. "You choose the book. But not the one about I like jam."

"We haven't got that one," she said. "We have the one about the bear hunt. It's for little kiddies really, but I like it."

She pulled my arm around her shoulder and settled the book across our knees, and we read it together.

When I was leaving, she pulled my head down and whispered in my ear. "It was my mam," she said, and put her hand to her face, which still bore the yellowing trace of a bruise.

"Oh," I said sympathetically. "So that's why you had to run away?"

"Yeah. We didn't want to be drawing *attention*. That's what Jonathan said."

"Right," I said.

"Bye-bye," she whispered, as if it were a secret.

"I'll come again," I said, and she nodded.

So that explained it. Up to a point.

Light Dawns

"He owes you big time," Emma said, when I reported back about visiting Julie.

"What do you mean?"

"Well, he disappears, we don't know whether he's alive or dead."

"We did know, though," I argued. "He sent a few texts."

"Yeah, but only rubbish ones."

"True," I said, "but we knew he was alive."

"All right. Technically, we knew he was alive. So he disappears off the face of the earth and we know he is alive but that is all we know, not a word of explanation, nothing, and he leaves you to . . . discover . . ."

She hesitated. She didn't want to say "the body", I'd say.

And anyway, he didn't leave me to discover it. How could he possibly know I was going to break in through his bathroom window?

"To deal with the fall-out," she amended. "You know. Then he expects you to turn up at the funeral . . ."

"He didn't expect it," I protested, but I don't think she even heard me.

". . . he gives you this big hug and everything, makes out you're practically engaged . . ."

This was such an exaggeration, all I could do was shake my head.

"And then he just disappears into thin air again. And then what does he do? He sends along this duck-shaped person with instructions about how you're to visit Julie. Please. He did say 'please', I take it?"

I nodded.

"And you say he's not your boyfriend, you're not together or anything?"

I shook my head.

"Hmm. So what do you do? You go and see the kid, and I know she's a little cutie and everything, and she starts doling out wisdom and tissues and upsets the hell out of you . . ."

"She didn't upset me."

"You're upset, Annie. Believe me, I know when you're upset."

"Shaken, maybe," I said. "But not upset."

"I bet she made you talk about your mam?"

I said nothing to that.

"I knew it," she said. "So she's upset you by asking you those questions that a *reasonable* person, i.e. a person-not-a-child, knows are taboo."

"What are you talking about, Emma? Taboo? What's taboo? What do you mean?"

"Oh, Annie! Listen to yourself. Just listen! You're so buttoned-up about your mother. It's a taboo subject, a no-go area. Everyone knows that. Everyone goes tiptoeing around that one, nobody ever mentions it, because you give out these 'Don't-go-there, don't-even-think-about-it' vibes as soon as the word 'mother' is mentioned . . ."

I swallowed hard.

"I've talked to you about her," I said.

"A bit," she said, "but you never really said anything."

That was news to me.

Well, OK, so maybe I did find it hard to talk about her.

"So where was I?" Emma went on. "Oh, yes, so Jonathan Kinahan swans out of your life, leaves you holding one hell of a baby, and then he swans back in again with a hug, and this request that you babysit his kid sister, and you, you great oaf of a lovesick cow, you do it. You go around there, you face that little Danielle monster in passing, not to mention Turdface, and, oh, Annie, you are so goddamn brave!"

I swallowed again. I was dumbstruck by all this. One minute I'm all taboos, and then I'm brave.

"I am just saying that he owes you big time. He owes you

an explanation. He owes you a thank-you. And he definitely owes you a phone call. He has owed you a phone call for ages, but now he most definitely does, and if he doesn't ring you soon, I think you should—"

"STOP!" I screeched.

I couldn't take any more of this tirade.

"What brought this on?" I asked, when Emma did eventually stop.

"Oh, the whole thing, Annie. I hate to see you so distressed."

"I'm not," I said.

"You are doing a very good imitation of it, then," she said.

"Well, I was, but I'm not now, I'm . . . improving."

"And going to see Julie . . ."

"That's *de*-stressing, Emma, not *dis*tressing. I feel much better since I saw her."

"Oh!" she said, deflating visibly. "Oh, right. Sorry. I thought . . . Well, that's good. But he still . . ."

"Owes me. OK, maybe so. But, Emma, he has just buried his mother."

"Even bereaved people can make phone calls," Emma said huffily.

"And he's in some . . . kind of *prison* place."

"That's just old Butler Butt talk," said Emma. "I'm sure he's not. He's only fourteen."

"Well, I think he must be, because he's not in foster care with Julie, which you'd think he would be, wouldn't you?"

"Hmm," she said.

"And he's not able to see Julie much, which is why he asked me to visit her."

"Which, by the way, he has no business asking you to do."

She was off again. I had to haul her back.

"Yes he has, Emma. Yes he has. What is a friend for, a really good friend, if you can't ask them to help you when you're in a fix, and Jono is definitely in a fix, no two ways about it."

"Hmm," said Emma again, but I could see that she was calming down a bit, was beginning to come around to my way of thinking.

"So you're trying to tell me you're flattered that he asked you . . ."

"I am trying to tell you that he is treating me like his best friend. And that is something I am glad to be."

"Hmm. I suppose."

We sat in silence for a while.

Then Emma said, "Well, now that you've done this thing for him, Annie, I think it is time you admitted that there is . . . that you two are . . . well, there is a relationship, right?"

I nodded slowly.

"OK, that's progress. So in that case, I think you should . . ."

"Yeah, I know, ring him. You've been saying that for ever."

"Or write to him, why don't you? If that's easier for you."

"I don't know where he is."

"But Ducky does. You could write to him care of her, couldn't you?"

A light dawned.

"Oh, yeah," I said. "I could do that. Maybe I will."

So I did.

Dear Jonathan

I don't know why you wanted me to visit your sister, but I did it anyway, since you asked, and when I actually went I was really glad because she is a tonic. When they say that about people, they usually mean they are a great gas, but she is more like an actual tonic like you take to jizz you up because you are feeling low. It is hard to feel low around Julie, even if you have a lot to feel low about, but I won't go into all that now. And you probably know anyway.

Please write back, or ring, I need to know that you are OK. And it would be nice to know where you are also, if that is not classified information.

Love from
Annie

Chapter 22

Heart-shaped Diamond

There was this ring on my dressing table. I don't wear rings myself, but if I did, they would be big and funky with mad stones like chunks of turquoise or gobs of rose quartz. But this wasn't funky. It was a proper grown-up ring, dainty and expensive-looking, with a heart-shaped diamond. I didn't know you could get diamonds cut like that. I had the feeling I'd seen it somewhere before.

I put it on my finger. It was a bit loose, but it looked lovely. It made me feel rich and beautiful.

I heard a shuffle behind me and turned around. Dad was standing in the doorway, watching me. He was clearly the person who'd put the ring there, judging by the beam on his face.

I held out the hand with the ring on it to him. The diamond winked in a beam of light that fell from a skylight we have on our landing.

"It's very pretty," I said. "Suits me, don't you think? But I can't marry you, Dad, that would be illegal."

He laughed. Then he took my hand and kissed my knuckle just above the ring. Very Prince Charming

"It's Mam's engagement ring," I said, "isn't it?"

He nodded.

"Dad, is that what was in the envelope?"

He nodded again. "You don't mind?"

I suppose he meant about giving me the ring, even though I'd said I didn't want it.

"Why didn't you tell me that's what it was?"

"You wouldn't let me. You went all white and horrified."

"Because I thought it was a letter, Dad. I didn't want a letter. I couldn't face that."

"Oh!" he said. "What made you think . . . ?"

"Envelope. Letter. Kind of logical?"

He laughed again. "Anyway, are you pleased?"

"I'm too young for it."

"Of course you are. I don't expect you to want to wear it. But are you glad to have it?"

"Of course, Dad. Thank you."

"She wanted you to have it."

OK, OK, so that is not earth-shattering. Mothers do want their daughters to inherit their jewels. But it was kind of nice all the same. If not in the jam league.

I smiled at him.

"So that's a start, then?" he said.

"What do you mean?"

"I mean, maybe you might start forgiving your mother, Annie."

This was heading towards the embarrassing end of the spectrum again, so I said, "Are you *bribing* me, Dad?"

He winced.

"Why are you so bitter, Annie?"

He put a hand to the side of his face in a despairing kind of gesture that made my heart contract.

"Sorry, Dad," I whispered.

"Annie," he said, "you can't measure love. It's not like sugar or petrol."

"*What?*"

I wasn't planning to make a bomb, for God's sake..

"Love doesn't come in kilos or litres, Annie," he persisted. "It doesn't come in amounts at all. There isn't more love or less love. It's a verb, not a noun. You do it. You create it. You give it. You build it. You share it. That's how it grows."

"What are you trying to say, Dad?" I asked.

He'd got the grammar all wrong, for a start.

"You heard me," he said. "Love is very powerful, Annie. But it can't cure cancer or stop a train. It doesn't work like that."

Well, thanks for that, I felt like saying, but I didn't.

"She was very sick, Annie. That's all."

"Simple as that," I said. I didn't mean to sound sarcastic. I really was trying.

"Of course not," he said. "It is not simple at all. But there is no need to make it more complicated than it already is."

"Yes, Dad," I said, and I kissed him. "Sorry."

"Annie," he said with a sigh. "Ann-*nie*. Go easy on yourself."

"Oh!"

I twisted the ring. For luck.

"Scrambled eggs for tea, then?" he said, suddenly all cheery.

I left the ring on my finger as I followed him down the stairs.

Chapter 23

Whatever the Opposite of a Suicide Note Is

I suppose the thing is, it's the alive people you have to rely on. In my case, mostly Dad. But Emma too. And even Julie. Not to mention her brother. And mine.

I thought about what Julie had said.

And I thought about what Emma had said.

And I thought about how Jono still hadn't said anything.

And then I wrote this letter.

Dear Mam

This wasn't Dr Thing's idea. I haven't been talking to Emma about this either, in case that is what you are thinking, so there is no pop psychology in here or anything. This is just what I have been working out for myself in my own head.

First off, I want you to know I am all right and second off I am not blaming you and I am not blaming myself either. I did do both of those things, I suppose, everyone does it, it's normal, but I have got over that. Just so we're clear.

See, the problem was, I was imagining you in black and white. That was where I went wrong. I have this thing about remembering black-and-white things like dreams and old movies in colour, but for some reason, I turned that talent inside out (without meaning to, I didn't even realize I was doing it) and I remembered you in black and white, and I know that can be very effective and moody and all the rest, but sometimes it can just be blurry, and that was the problem.

And not only were you all blurry, I was all blurry too. Which is the opposite of what you would expect, you would think that you know yourself very well, but actually, it's like looking too close up at a thing, you can't see it whole, only the details, and that is how I have been seeing myself, I think. Not that that is a problem, I'm only saying.

Remembering everything in black and white really sucks, so from now on, I am really going to try to remember in colour, and then I think it might be more authentic. I like the idea of authenticity. It is the best idea. Authenticity rocks. It is like truth, but not exactly, it's more a particular kind of truth. Like, it is true that six of one is the same as half a dozen of the other, as old Mrs Kinahan used to say, but it is authentic if I remember scenes as they actually felt. That is probably not a very developed idea, but I am young yet. I am working on it.

Look, if we are being authentic here, and I don't know about you, but I am trying anyway, I do have to say my life has not exactly been a picnic since that day. But, hey, we can't always be on picnics, can we? I have got very philosophical, you will have noticed. In both senses.

I don't exactly believe in heaven, but on the other hand, I definitely believe in hell, because I've had a few little glimpses in there, so logically I should really conclude that there is a heaven too. I will go so far as to say that I believe, as Mr O'Connell told me the other day, that there are more things in heaven and earth, Horatio, than are dreamt of in your philosophy (which doesn't mean your philosophy, apparently, it means, yer philosophy, as in this philosophy lark generally). And Horatio is neither here nor there. Also, this is from a completely different play than the one we are reading this year, which I told Mr O I thought was muddying the waters, but he said, "Annie, the waters are for muddying." (This wasn't an English class. He doesn't teach me. This was just a conversation. He is that kind of person.)

So there you go. Life is complicated. I wouldn't have it any other way.

In any case, I have no idea if you will ever have the slightest inkling about what I am writing to you, but I thought I would write it down anyway. I don't know what I will do with this letter, though. Maybe burn it. Ceremonially. Like sending a Santa letter up the chimney.

So this is really just to say Hi, and I'm here, and I'm reasonably OK, and I'm going to keep on doing the colouring-in.

Give my love to the angels.
Miss you

Annie

That was a bit mean about putting Emma and pop psychology in the same sentence. I don't even think that. But the good thing is, she will never know. Because I am definitely going to burn the letter.

Love Text

I'm all letters these days.

But sending that letter to Jono was the best thing. (Thanks, Emma.) Because I finally got a text from him that was not about football.

It was about *LOVE*!!!!

> "Love me and leave me not."
> Merchant, act 5, scene 1
> J

Love me and leave me not. That made me jump. Well, it made me furrow my brow anyway. What could he mean, Love him and leave him not? I'm not going anywhere, I'm not leaving anyone. I'm here, I'm still here, I'm the one that stays in the same place.

It struck me that if I could have sent that message to *her* . . . she might still be here, mightn't she, if I'd said something like that to her, if I'd thought to say it. *Love me and leave me not.*

I know, I know, *it's never the little girl's fault*, but still, you can't help thinking, can you? You can't help thinking, if only . . . maybe if . . . suppose I'd . . . And most of the time you can't decide what should be in there where the dots are, how you might finish the thought, finish the sentence, and then someone comes along and says something like *Love me and leave me not* and suddenly you're filling in the gaps for yourself, you're thinking, That's *it*, maybe if I could have got through to her, if I'd said something, if she'd known I didn't want her to go, if I'd just *said*, "Love me." Or, "Don't leave me."

But I didn't know she was going anywhere. It isn't really the kind of thing you discuss with people, because if you did, the first thing they are going to do is tell you not to do it, and they would probably have all these really logical reasons about why you shouldn't do it, and you wouldn't want to hear that, because you wouldn't be thinking logically, would you? You would just be wanting to stop whatever is going on in your head and making you feel so *desperate*. You'd want the frondy things to stop wrapping themselves around your ankles, you'd want your breath to stop sticking in your lungs. You'd want it all just to stop, *stop*, STOP.

And even love can't stop a train.

So then I said to Dr Thing, "I found her."

He dropped his pencil altogether when he heard that.

"I found my mother," I repeated.

He picked his pencil up again and he gave a satisfied little nod. And then it struck me. He'd *known* all along.

Daaaaad!

But I suppose he had to tell, and it doesn't matter now anyway.

"I was eight years old," I went on. "Or maybe nine. Or ten. What does it matter, I was only a little kid. I came home from school one day and I rang the doorbell and nobody answered. I'd . . . yes, I think . . . I'd forgotten my key. 'No-key' was my middle name."

Dr Thing said, "You're sure about that, Annie? You're not thinking about the other time?"

I hesitated.

"Yes," I said eventually. "I was always losing my key or forgetting it."

But I was sure now, about the key.

"I thought I'd lost it, only then . . . I found it. I had . . . I had one of those old-fashioned satchel schoolbags. It had belonged to my aunt or someone when they were little, and I'd found it in the attic and I wanted to have it because I had seen pictures of children in the sixties wearing bags like that, so I took my bag off my back." It was coming back faster than I could tell it. "I took all the books and copies out of it, and in the very bottom corner, I found the key, and I stood up on tippy-toes and I opened the door and I went in.

"It was deathly quiet in the house and . . . I thought she was asleep, because she was in bed, in her pyjamas, but she was very cold, so I put an extra blanket over her and then I went and had my tea, and my dad came home and I told him I couldn't wake Mam up."

The blanket.

That was the blanket. I mean, that was when I put the blanket . . . not the other time. Oh!

"Well *done*, Annie," said Dr Thing very quietly.

"Its not fair," I said then. "It's not *fair.* That's twice it happened to the same person. *Me.*"

"No, Annie," he said. "It's not fair."

"But it is never the little girl's fault, is it?"

I looked up at him and I felt about seven years old.

"Who told you that?" he asked.

My heart shot across my body like a lightning bolt.

"You mean, it *might* be?"

"No, no, I don't mean that. I just mean, it sounds like something someone said to you, because it is not the way you usually talk, is all."

"Julie told me," I said.

"Who is Julie?" he asked.

"A little girl I know."

"I see," he said. Though I can't for the life of me know how he could see. It's just a thing people say.

"So am I cured?" I asked. "Doctor."

"I don't know," he said. "Were you sick?"

"I don't know," I said.

"How do you feel?" he asked.

"I feel all right," I said.

"And did you feel all right all along?"

"No," I said.

"Any idea when you started to feel all right?"

"No," I said.

Though I had, really, It started with the jam memory. And then there was going to see Julie. And then there was writing to Jono. And to Mam.

"But you do feel all right?"

"Yeah," I said.

"Time will tell," he said.

"I suppose it will," I said. "Thanks, Doc. And goodbye."

"You're a star, Annie," he said, as he opened the door for me.

Promotion from starfish! Hey!

The Blanket

I shot up in bed.

The blanket!

I'd told the guard that I'd put a blanket over Jono's mother, but that wasn't right. It was my own mother that I'd put the blanket over. I'd mixed up the two memories.

I lay down again, my heart still pounding and the sweat evaporating on my skin.

Think, I said to myself. Think.

The guard had asked me very specifically if I'd put a blanket over her, and I hadn't. The blanket had been there already. Yes, there was definitely a blanket over her.

How come?

It must have been Jono who did that.

So what did that mean? Was it a good thing or a bad thing that he'd put the blanket over her?

It meant he definitely knew she was there on the floor. He didn't just run off with Julie thinking their mother was safely tucked up in her bed. And why had they run away?

Stop, I said to myself. *Stop thinking about that part, and concentrate on the blanket.*

OK, so he put the blanket over her. She was asleep on the floor, or passed out drunk, or concussed or whatever, and he put the blanket over her.

Right, so that meant she wasn't dead when he left, right? Because you don't put a blanket over a dead person – unless you are eight years old and think you can warm then up.

You might put a sheet over a dead person, but that's different, that's to hide their face, and the blanket wasn't like that, it was just thrown over her, the way you'd throw a rug over a sleeping person. So. Jono definitely thought his mother was asleep. He must have.

And he must have told the police he'd done that. He must have said, *She was asleep, and I threw a blanket over her.*

Oh Lord God.

And then I'd come along and said *I* had put the blanket over her. They thought that was important, because they double-checked. So they thought Jono was lying.

I've *incriminated* him. By mistake.

I sat up in bed again, panic coursing through my veins.

Lie down, I said to myself. *Calm down. It's the middle of the night. You can ring the station in the morning and explain.*

I couldn't sleep, though.

In the end I put on my dressing gown and I went and woke Dad up.

"You *goof-head,*" he said when I told him the story.

"It's much worse than a goof!" I wailed. "Dad, they have probably put Jono in prison because of me. They probably think he . . ."

"They just think he told a lie," Dad said. "Or was confused.

It doesn't make him a criminal, Annie. And he is not in prison. Where did you get that idea?"

"No, but they'll think he is a criminal. They'll think he said he put a blanket over her to convince them that he didn't know she was dead."

"No, Annie, they won't think that. It's too far-fetched. Think it through," Dad said calmly. "He claims to have put a blanket over her, he tells them he did that, but he hasn't done it, he's made it up, but then by complete chance someone else comes along and puts a blanket over her, making his lie seem plausible? That can't be right. It's ridiculous."

"But they thought it was important," I argued. "They came around specially to check about the blanket."

"Because it was a puzzle. They were just checking out his story, asking you if you'd seen the blanket, and then you threw a spanner in the works by claiming it was you who had put the blanket on her. That's a loose end, it doesn't make sense. But it's not going to make them accuse Jonathan of anything, Annie. And in any case, we'll phone them first thing in the morning and tell them and then it will be all right. Go to sleep now, like a good girl."

I shuffled back to bed, but I didn't sleep a wink. I kept

imagining Jono in some awful prison somewhere, slopping out and not allowed any visitors, all because I'd misled the police.

We went straight to the station after breakfast and I made a statement and they said that was fine, thank you, and they didn't look a bit concerned, so maybe Dad was right after all.

So maybe I didn't actually save Jonathan or anything by my heroic act of owning up, but I like to think I helped.

Come on, fair's fair.

And I definitely felt better after it.

Chapter 26

Making It All Go Heart-shaped

I dreamed it again, the night after the blanket panic, the seaweedy nightmare, where I am being grabbed and strangled by wafty things under water, like ribbony fingers.

But I told myself, I'm a *starfish*. I've got an *exo*-skeleton.

I don't know where starfish swim, down near the seabed, or up near the surface, but in the dream, I made myself swim with all five starfishy arms, swim and swim and swim and swim and swim, up, up, up, up, up, and away from all those wafty, frondy, ribbony things, and away from those big black sucky holes.

I swam to the surface of my dream and I drank in the sweet, sweet air. *In such a night as this* . . . I woke.

Love me and leave me not.

I am not going anywhere, Jonathan, I thought, and I reached out for my phone and looked again at that text he had sent:

> "Love me and leave me not."
> Merchant, act 5, scene 1
> J

Merchant. That had to be the play we're doing at school, I thought, *The Merchant of Venice*. Mr O must be doing it with his class too, then, because he is Jono's English teacher. Act Five has to be near the end. He really must have a lot of time on his hands, Jono, if he'd got that far. (*Prison!* I thought, and gulped.)

I got up then and went and got my copy of the play and I opened it up at Act Five, scene one. There *is* only one scene in Act Five (that's a cheat), but it's a long one. I found the bit about 'Love me and leave me not' and it's engraved on a ring! (Oh, wow, a ring!)

And then I found Dr Thing's favourite bit, right at the beginning of Act Five. "The moon shines bright." (By the way, why isn't it 'brightly'? Maybe it's a poetic licence thing. I suppose if you are Shakespeare, you are allowed to break the grammar rules.)

So I texted Jono back and said:

> I'm not going anywhere, in such a night as this.
> How about you? A

I didn't know if he would get the "in such a night" bit, but I didn't care. I liked putting it in anyway.

After that, I slept again. Really well.

And then I woke in the morning to the sharp *beep-beep* of a text message coming in on my mobile:

> I'm coming back to school next week.
> WYGOWM? J

Coming back to school. So he *wasn't* in prison. He *couldn't* be, because they don't let you out of prison to go to school, I know that much. That *bloody* Turdface Butler.

I had to Google the last bit of Jono's text message. I didn't know what it meant. I have never been asked out by text before. As soon as I found out, I tapped in, as fast as I could, and sent it before I had time to think:

Yes. C u soon.
Love u lots,
Annie

x x x x
x x x
x x
x x
x x
x

Emma showed me how to make the heart shape. Like I said, Emma knows *everything*. I don't care if Val's Day was, like, weeks ago. The heart knows no time limits.

PS

I don't really think you can actually die from eating too many bananas. You would have to eat so many of them to get potassium poisoning, you'd explode first. Which would also kill you, of course, but, hey, come on.

All the same, eating too many bananas is not to be recommended. (Don't do this at home, children.) Same goes for nuts, cough lozenges, yoghurt, bread, chocolate, stew, blueberries, fish fingers, cake, pasta, mustard, figs, ice cream, Smarties, smoothies, jam . . .

Things I realize I have been getting wrong about my mother (RIP), now that I know it's never the little girl's fault

1 She hated me. (Of course she didn't hate me. I never really thought that, I just liked saying it, because it made everything simpler.)
2 I hated her. (Well, she did annoy the socks off me sometimes, but that is how things *are* in families.)
3 She loved Jamie more. (Ah, God, that's so pathetic it's not even worth commenting on.)
4 She did it because of me. (How important do I bloody think I bloody am?)
5 She had a reason for doing it. (Something made her do it, obviously, but it's not a *reason*able thing, it's all about mixed-up emotion, so even trying to think reasonably about it is pointless, like trying to use algebra to work out grammar.)
6 I could have prevented it. (Rubbish. And ditto re: How important . . . etc., see above.)

My favourite shapes

5 Ring
4 Diamond
3 Polka dot
2 Star
1 Heart

If you enjoyed this novel and are wondering what is going on in Jonathan's life, you might like to read the companion novel, *Bruised* . . .

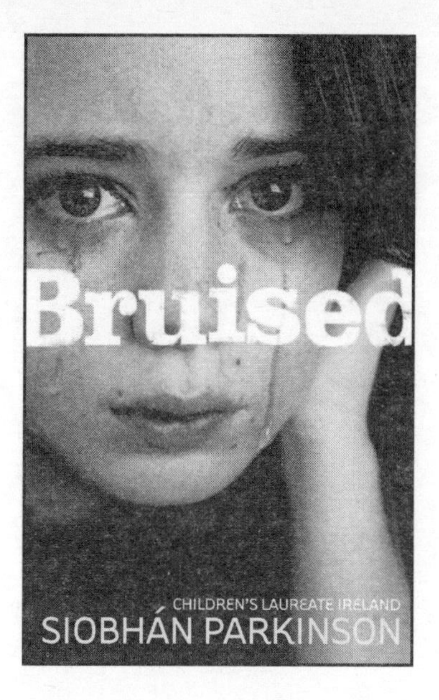

The idea for BRUISED began to form in Siobhán Parkinson's mind when she heard a woman on the radio telling the story of her childhood with an alcoholic mother. One day, when there was no food in the house, the mother had come home with a bag of apples for the children's dinner. "What struck me," says Parkinson, "was how that one incident had such a hold on the adult who had been that child. Many things had happened in that house that were much more shocking than being given only apples for your dinner, but somehow those apples had become a metaphor for all the abuse and neglect she had suffered in childhood. I mulled over that image of the apples for years, and then one day, I remembered a question a little girl had asked me once at a reading in Dublin: 'Would you ever think of writing a book where the mammy dies?'That sad little question, which went to my heart at the time, began to rattle around in my head along with the apples, and a few lines that my nephew had been quoting from *The Merchant of Venice*, which he was reading at school – and suddenly it all fell into place, and I began to write a story about a brother and sister, Jono and Julie, who live with an alcoholic mother, in a home where the love has gone bad."